CHAPTER ONE

Sweat dripped from Fraser's swollen brow, collecting blood from the cut above his eye then fell to his knee, ran down his leg and discoloured his white sock. In the one minute break between rounds, Fraser tried to control his heart rate, but all around him was a fear-inducing blur of taunts, shouts, bright lights and abuse. Ahead of him, in the far corner, his opponent, Mackie, sat staring back at him while his trainer held up a water bottle to suck at.

"Let's go, boys," called the ref, a middle-aged man dressed in a white shirt and black trousers that struggled to contain his excessive paunch. "Round five."

There was no bell. The audience didn't fill an arena. The ring was in the basement of a pub in Plaistow where bare-knuckle fighting provided high stakes for every villain worth his salt for miles around. But the bare-knuckle fights at the Golden Ring Pub had one major difference; they were no holds barred fights to the death.

Plaistow was Fraser's home turf. Mackie was the guest fighter, but he was good, and he had got in early with a debilitating blow to Fraser's sight in round two.

"Get a move on," called someone from the crowd behind Mackie.

"Yeah, get up and fight, you pussy," another shouted.

Mackie's red shorts were in the centre of the ring. Fraser could see them, rocking from side to side as his opponent bounced from foot to foot to stay warm and loose.

Fraser pushed off the ropes but held onto the ropes for a second. His vision was returning, or so he thought. He turned his head from side to side trying to focus on something, anything. Movement in the corner of his eye caused him to duck instinctively and Mackie's arm swung across the top of Fraser's head, grazing his shaved scalp. Fraser jabbed at his blurred shape, felt the connection, and followed through with a combination, the last of which glanced off Mackie's sweaty body and sent Fraser stumbling forward.

That was when he knew it was over.

A hook out of nowhere connected with Fraser's head. He raised his arms to block the attack, but it was too late. The blows came fast, hard and with relentless brutality. The gloveless, hammer-like punches finding their mark every time.

Three punches sealed the deal. The first to his temple slowed Fraser's world to a crawl. The second to his nose brought with it the familiar iron taste of his own blood. The third was an uppercut that shook the life from Fraser's mind and turned his world to a dance of swirling lights.

Darkness came as he hit the floor and felt the warm rush of adrenaline fighting a lost cause.

Spinning lights greeted Fraser when he woke. Angry shouts from the wild audience waned and dropped an octave as if someone had slowed time to a crawl.

"Finish him," yelled a man, who had climbed up onto the ropes and leaned into the ring.

But all Fraser could see was a dark silhouette above him that seemed to spin as if Fraser was laying on a turntable. The man's voice was rough and hoarse from shouting but carried authority. The man wasn't just a member of the audience; he was Del Dixon, the renowned South London gangster who managed Mackie.

STONE FIST

A STONE COLD THRILLER

J. D. WESTON

WESTON MEDIA

STONE FIST

"Mackie, get in there and finish it or I'll get in there and finish you myself."

More faces appeared at the ropes, keen to see the fight come to its ultimate conclusion.

Two knees dropped down onto Fraser's shoulders, slippery with sweat. The spinning slowed enough for Fraser to make out Mackie's blurred form.

For a moment, the two fighters locked eyes, sharing some kind of kindred understanding.

Fraser understood what Mackie had to do. He was ready.

He nodded once and closed his eyes before Mackie delivered his final blows. The first was a hook that forced Fraser's head to one side, ripping his neck muscle and breaking some teeth. But the pain was short-lived. The second blow crushed Fraser's temple against the canvas floor of the ring, fracturing his skull. The third broke his jaw.

The fourth punch turned the lights out for Fraser, but enough consciousness remained for him to hear the taunting, muffled count of five, six and seven, before Mackie's final punch opened Fraser's fractured skull and consciousness leaked away like bloodied water into a drain.

CHAPTER TWO

"What are you going to do, John?" asked Mick, as he handed John a tumbler of brandy. "You can't pull out now. There's only a few days until the next fight. Dixon will start a bleeding war if you pull out now."

"I'm aware of the time constraints, Mick. I'm thinking. Can't you see I'm bleeding thinking?" replied John Cooper. He loosened the collar of his tailored shirt and ran his hand through his silver brush of short hair.

"I reckon Dixon's boys got to him before the fight," said Mick. He paced the floor of John Cooper's office, swirling his brandy and trying to put the images of Fraser's crushed skull to the back of his mind. "I mean, he was a dead cert. Never lost a fight. Never been knocked down. And in one bleeding fight, the most important of his life, he goes and gets himself killed. It doesn't make sense, John."

"So what do you suggest then, Mick? You seem to have all the answers. What do you suggest we do? I just lost two hundred grand on a dead cert. If I pull out now, I'll lose another three." He fumbled with his silver cufflinks and rolled his sleeves to show an aged but tanned and toned pair of forearms. John had worked his way up the ranks. He'd done his share of dirty work. Being so close to losing it all over a fight was not part of his master plan.

Mick eyed him above the rim of his brandy glass.

"If you've got a plan, Mick, now's the time to mention it."

"Only one thing we can do, John," he replied, matching John's tone, a trait he knew he respected. He returned to his pacing, a habit John recognised as Mick running scenarios in his head, seeing all angles. "Make sure we don't bleeding lose. If we win the next one, we'll be three hundred grand up."

"Don't give me ifs, Mick. Ifs aren't going to give me a boner. Ifs aren't going to put money in my bleeding pocket, are they?" He sank his drink and held up his glass for Mick to refill. His number two might know how to talk to him, but he still had to be put in his place every now and again. "No. No, what we need is a dead cert."

Mick span back to face him. The long tails of his three-quarter length jacket followed shortly after.

"With all due respect, John, Fraser *was* a dead cert."

"Fraser wasn't a dead cert. He was a loser, Mick. No family. No obligations. And he had more debt than Greece. What do you think he was thinking when the fight started going pear-shaped for him? He wasn't thinking of his wife and kids, was he? No, he wasn't. There was nothing to make him try harder."

"Nothing worth fighting for, you mean?" said Mick.

"Exactly. He knew what he was up for and he knew who he was up against. As far as Fraser was concerned, if he won, he'd have fifty grand in his bin to blow on hookers and coke, or he'd have been killed. Either way, he couldn't care less."

"So we need someone who's married?"

"Not necessarily married, Mick. But someone with a few more scruples. Who have we got?"

"Bill Jackson. He's not married, but he's got a couple of kids."

"No, he's a mincer. He dances about too much. I'm not having three hundred bags of sand sitting on someone who can't keep bleeding still for three seconds, let alone stand in a ring and have the crap beaten out of them."

"How about Fox?"

"Stan Fox?" said John, dismissing the idea before Mick could even make an argument. "When was the last time he fought?"

"I don't know, but word is out that he's training again and in good shape, by all accounts."

"No, Mick, be serious. Stan Fox is an alcoholic. All Dixon would need to do to convince him to go down in the first round would be to tell him there's a bottle of vodka in hell with his name on it, and he'd flop before the bleeding bell rang."

"There must be someone, John," said Mick, handing him another brandy.

"Why haven't we thought about this sooner?" asked John. "I mean, we put five hundred grand on the table, two for the first fight, three for the second. And we haven't got any contingency? Why the bleeding hell not?"

"Well, John, Fraser was a dead cert, right? You even said it your-self once. You wouldn't even enter into the bet if we didn't have Fraser."

"Yes, Mick, but Fraser, in case you hadn't noticed, just had his head caved in by some South London bleeding pikey, and if we don't have a replacement for the fight in two weeks' time and I have to hand over three hundred more of my hard-earned grands, I'll be caving your bleeding head in."

"Alright, John, alright. We'll sort it, okay?"

"No, Mick, it's certainly not alright. Alright is certainly not what it is. Here's what I want you to do."

"Go on, John. Anything. You name them, I'll find them."

"No, Mick. We're not going to use anyone we know. Dixon will be one step ahead. We can't have the slimy little bastard getting to them before the fight, and we don't know who he's already got to, do we? No, we don't."

"So who then, John?"

"Someone new, Mick. Fresh blood."

"Where the bleeding hell am I supposed-"

"On the streets, Mick. Find me someone."

"Someone married, yeah?"

"What I need, Mick, is someone who can stand in the ring with the hardest pikey I've ever seen. Someone who we can offer a carrot to. And someone who might have a thing or two to lose."

"I'm on it, John. I'll talk to Nigel down the gym. He might-"

"You'll talk to no-one, Mick. Take Jack with you."

"Jack's a bit of a loose cannon, John."

"Even more reason to take him with you."

"Got it," said Mick. "I'll go get him now and call you with what we find." He sank his drink, put his glass down and opened the door.

"I'll tell you what you're going to find, Mick," said John.

Mick turned at the door and raised his eyebrows, waiting for John to finish.

"You're going to find me a dead cert."

CHAPTER THREE

The morning dew that clung to the wild grass soaked Harvey's feet and legs with every stride he took. Wispy leaves and branches whipped at his face as he tore through the brush and clean, fresh air filled his lungs with every rhythmic breath.

The early morning fog hung across his neighbour's field, blocking his view of the beach and the sea when he broke free of the forest and ran into the soft mud that stuck to his boots and doubled their weight. The three-hundred metre stretch of dirt that ran alongside the field to the beach road was littered with potholes. Only when Harvey had launched himself over the small hedgerow, run across the old tarmac and reached the sandy beach did he open himself up for the final sprint along the water's edge. A full five-hundred metre sprint.

Harvey passed the old man who swam naked in the cold sea each morning. He waved mid-sprint as he did every day, then slowed for the five-minute jog home. Only when he reached his driveway did Harvey start to walk and warm down. He stretched, kicked the mud off his boots then entered his house by the back door, which opened into the kitchen.

He tossed four small logs into the wood-burner then, from a metal pail he kept beside the fire, he grabbed a handful of dried kindling and made a small pile inside the stove. He lit a match, waited for the kindling to ignite, and then moved two of the logs either side of the flame. It didn't take long for the oils in the pine to find the flames. He closed the door and stripped off. Before he went to the bathroom, he poured a jug of water into the cast iron kettle that sat on the burner and left it to boil.

With no hot water in the pipes until the wood-burner had been running for thirty minutes, Harvey took his usual cold shower. It was a habit he'd formed from necessity. He'd heard stories of macho characters in films like James Bond who took cold showers because it made them feel alive and woke their senses so they could operate at full efficiency. For Harvey, he'd been for a run and needed a shower, so he took one. It was simple.

He had just stepped in when the door to the bathroom opened. The movement was caught in the corner of his eye, but he turned away, pretending not to see. In the reflection of the chrome shower rail, a shadow passed behind him, slow and stealthy. He continued to rinse the mud from his short, dark hair, counting down all the while and gauging the timing of the attack until he was sure his assailant's hand would be just inches away.

He turned and grabbed a wrist, twisting it up and backwards so their body fell into his, and dragged Melody into the shower screaming from the sharp sting of the freezing cold water. Soaked in her nightdress and with water dripping from her hair, she wrapped herself in a towel, cursing him.

"One day, Harvey Stone," she said. "One day, you won't see me coming."

Harvey didn't reply. He turned his back on her, finished rinsing his body, and switched the water off. Taking the towel that Melody offered him, Harvey stepped out. Melody edged backwards out of the room, smiling at him.

"Go and stand by the fire," said Harvey. "It'll be hot by now."

"I'd rather stand here watching you," she replied. "I missed this."

"You missed what? Launching an unsuccessful attack on me and having your morning ruined by a cold shower?"

"I wouldn't change it for the world. What did you do when..."

"When what, Melody?" asked Harvey. "When we were split up?"

"Yeah. What was life like for you? How was it different?"

"It was the same as it is now," replied Harvey, as he turned to face Melody. "There was only really one major difference to my life."

"Oh," she said, biting her lower lip, "and was it something to do with what we did last night?"

"No," said Harvey, wrapping the towel around his waist and preparing for another attack. "I had to make my own coffee."

As Melody's face dropped and she whipped her towel at him, the kettle on the wood-burner began to whistle.

"Timed to perfection, Mr Stone."

"We've got a long drive ahead of us. We need coffee."

Melody continued the conversation from the open kitchen-lounge area, shouting through to Harvey as he dressed.

"I still can't believe Reg is getting married. After all these years, he's never struck me as the type, you know?"

"He's happy. I think we both owe the guy more credit than he gets. Let him have his moment," he replied, as he walked into the kitchen, pulling a clean t-shirt over his head.

"How many times?" asked Melody, as she handed him a coffee then reached for her own.

"How many times what?"

"How many times do you think he's saved your life?" asked Melody. "I mean, all the dumb things you've done, all the broken bones and nearly getting yourself blown up, and Reg has taken care of us from behind his laptop, sitting in a van."

"Too many times," said Harvey, as he stoked the fire with two more logs. "Too many times."

CHAPTER FOUR

"Left jab, right jab, hook. Left jab, right jab, hook," said Old Man McGee, leaning into the pads as Tyler followed his commands. "Watch my feet. Watch my feet. Lead with your right. Right jab, left hook. Faster, Tyler. Right jab, left hook. Watch my feet. Watch for the change. Too slow. Back to basics. Left jab, right jab, hook. Left jab, right jab, hook. Good. Watch for my feet to change. Look at my eyes. You don't need to look at my feet to see them move."

Tyler held McGee's eyes and dealt him the required moves, hard and fast.

"Move, Tyler. You're flat-footed. Get me up against the ropes. I'm moving, Tyler. Follow me. Left jab, right jab, hook. Watch my feet. Are you tired?"

Tyler watched the pads dance in front of him. He bounced from foot to foot and landed the three punch combination.

"Get your weight behind it. Come on, Tyler. You're a big boy. Move with it."

Another combination hit the pads. Three successful blows. Three vibrating exhales that matched the dull thuds like a snare drum with a bass.

"Right, good," said McGee. "Let's call it a day. Get washed up."

The old man shook the pads off his hands. Tyler turned to Lloyd, who stood beside the ring to help remove his gloves.

"You did good, Tyler," said Lloyd. His voice hit the lower octaves that seemed to be reserved for men of African descent. "Listen to the old man. Do what he says. He's putting time into you. Respect that. When he says move your feet, move your feet. When he says put your weight behind the punch, he means it. You won't hurt him. I've seen bigger guys than you in here, and the old man would put them all on their arses with a look when they don't do what he says."

"Yeah, I know," said Tyler. He turned and watched McGee pick up a broom and sweep the floor beneath the row of six-foot punch bags that hung from the ceiling joists. "He knows his stuff. Did he train you?"

Lloyd gave a laugh through his nose like a single note on a tuba.

"No, but I've been ringside long enough to know a good one from a bad one," said Lloyd, as he pulled off the first glove.

"A good trainer, you mean?" said Tyler, flexing his hand.

"A good man." He nodded at Old Man McGee. "And that right there is about as good as they get. Do you see anyone else in here tonight?"

"Well, no, but I guess it's late."

"How many gyms have you trained in?" asked Lloyd.

"Enough."

"Were they ever empty?"

"Well, not really. There were always one or two guys there."

"The old man's putting time into you. Right now, you're his focus. You want my advice?"

"Yeah, go on."

"Make the most of it. Don't let him down."

"I don't plan on letting anyone down, Lloyd," replied Tyler. "Did you fight?" He held out his left hand for Lloyd to untie.

"Yeah, I fought. Won some. Lost some. I just like being here."

"I know what you mean," said Tyler. "I've been in gyms since I was a boy. It's the smell that gets me. I don't think I'll ever forget that smell."

"Sweat?" asked Lloyd, as he pulled the glove.

"No, mate. Hard work." He winked at Lloyd who held the ropes open for Tyler to step through. "I'll shower up at home. See you tomorrow, yeah?"

"You sure will," said Lloyd.

The old man leaned on his broom as Tyler walked past.

"Thanks for tonight," said Tyler. "Same time tomorrow, yeah?"

"If you're game," said the old man. "I'll be here. Always am."

The sound of the brush strokes faded as the door closed behind Tyler, giving way to the sound of rain hitting the street. The gym was in the fourth arch along below a railway bridge. Dim street lights lit the road, but the path was dark and immersed in shadows, lit only by the reflection of the city on the surface of the water.

A few cars rolled past, creating small waves as they cut through the deep puddles of water. At the end of the road, Tyler turned left and made his way towards Shadwell. The walk home usually gave Tyler time to think about the things the old man had said about his technique, but it was Lloyd's words that accompanied Tyler that night. The fact that the old man had chosen to focus on him over all the others, it was motivating. It was his chance and he wouldn't let him down.

He passed tyre shops and garages, an old church, and small parks that were tiny pockets of green between rows of blocks of flats. An old factory that had been reclaimed and turned into high-end apartments marked the end of the council housing. A narrow road marked the division where offices took over, climbing higher towards the city. The division also marked Tyler's home, which was a small flat in a two-story high building. He was thankful for the location. Although he would have liked to have been closer to the gym, the council flats were a maze of gang fights, drugs and crime. The last thing Tyler needed was to be mixed up in anything.

"Mum?" he called, when he opened his front door. "Are you awake?"

No reply came. Tyler eased the front door closed, stepped into the kitchen, and flicked on the light.

On the sideboard was a plate with a knife and a mug. He washed them under the tap and turned them upside down on the draining board to dry. The kitchen, which overlooked the road below, had been painted in a sickly yellow. The ceiling had signs of mildew in the corners and the linoleum floor was torn by the door. The council provided the housing. His mother had been taken ill two years previously and had since been unable to work. Tyler took care of her between work and training. Although she was stubborn and determined to cook her own meals and bathe herself, some days the chemo cut her down and reduced her to a fraction of the woman Tyler remembered as a child.

Tyler used a cloth to wipe the sink clean, then folded it, hung it over the tap, and reached over the counter to close the two small curtains.

That was when he saw two men staring up at him from the street below.

CHAPTER FIVE

"Was that the best you've got, John?" Del Dixon's already hoarse voice was like gravel over the mobile connection. "Who are you putting up next? Your old lady?"

"Very witty, Del," replied John. "How did you do it?"

"Do what, John? I hope you're not accusing me of anything."

"There's no way Fraser lost his form overnight, Del."

"Choose your words carefully."

"I'll choose my words how I like, Del."

"So we're still on for the second match then? I mean, you're not going to run away?"

"I've given you two hundred grand, Del. I don't intend on losing any more."

"So tell me. Who are you putting up?"

"Why? What are you going to do? Pay them a visit? Are you going to send the boys round? I don't think so."

"You don't have anyone yet, do you?" said Dixon.

John remained silent.

"I'm right, aren't I? You're not your usual cocky self because right now you don't know who's going in that ring."

"I've been in this game a long time, Del. I can smell when a fighter has been got to. It smells like rotten flesh."

"Maybe you need a break from it all then, John. Maybe you've lost your touch. It's nothing to be ashamed of."

"I haven't lost anything."

"Except two hundred grand."

"I'm too long in the tooth for your games, Del."

"So we're on then, are we?" said Del. "Two weeks' time. Oh, and John?"

John let the silence speak for itself and waited for Del to continue.

"I prefer cash if you don't mind."

The call disconnected. John slid his phone onto his desk, picked up his tumbler of brandy and downed its contents. But Del's words played over in his mind. He imagined the self-righteous smile that accompanied the smug voice. John hurled his glass across the room. It smashed against the wall, sending tiny fragments of crystal glass to the solid oak floor, and left a tear of amber to run down the plaster.

He picked up the phone again and dialled Mick's number, who answered on the first ring.

"Give me good news," said John.

"Nothing confirmed yet. But we have two options, John. We're working on bringing them in."

"I want a name tonight and I want to meet them tomorrow. Make it happen, Mick."

He hung up the call before Mick could respond, then poured a fresh brandy into a new glass from the tray beside his desk. At the forefront of his thoughts was an image of Del handing over three hundred thousand pounds. A profit of one hundred thousand wasn't bad. But in the two-match run, the scores would be equal. One win each. A hundred thousand pounds didn't have the same ring to it as the original five hundred. Taking five hundred grand from Del Dixon would have set John back on top of the food chain. One hundred would just about make them even, once the damage to reputation had been factored in.

He tapped his phone against his lip, letting possibilities run amok like a roulette wheel inside his mind. Ideas were scratched off as they appeared. Having Del taken out was too risky, and he'd be expecting it, just as John was ready for a hit himself. Having Del's family taken out just wasn't how things were done. Families were a no go. It was an unwritten rule between men such as John and Del Dixon. Hitting his business was a possibility. But two weeks wasn't long enough to coordinate such an effort. The wheel span with just a few ideas remaining. It slowed, and the clicking sound slowed with it, until the pointer hung between two final ideas, both as dangerous as the other.

And then the wheel stopped.

With the last of the brandy in John's gullet, he dialled Del's number. He breathed in and savoured the air that cooled the alcohol burn inside his throat while he listened to the ringtone.

"Cooper?" said Del. "You're keen tonight. You've caught me counting my winnings, so make it quick."

"Double it," said John. "Six hundred grand."

A silence followed, broken only by the whisper of the telephone signal.

"Six hundred grand and the Golden Ring," said Dixon.

CHAPTER SIX

With a final glance around the house, Harvey committed the scene to memory. It was a trick he'd learned from his mentor, Julios. Each item, no matter how small or trivial, had been placed in such a way that any differences in position would stand out a mile on Harvey's return.

He pulled the back door closed, locked it, and then walked around to the front of the house, where Melody was waiting in her little sports car. The roof was down and their luggage was in the tiny back seat. She smiled as he approached and started the car. Harvey took a final look at the house then climbed into the passenger seat.

"Are you sure you don't want to drive?" asked Melody. "It's a long way to London."

The seat slid back as far as it would go and Harvey stretched his legs out.

"I'm good," he replied. "It's about time you earned your keep."

"You know what, Harvey Stone?" said Melody. "If I'm not mistaken, I do believe you're developing a sense of humour."

Harvey didn't reply. Instead, he watched the house disappear in the side-view mirror and let Melody ponder on her statement some more.

"Maybe it's just that you're relaxed," she mused. "You love that house, don't you?"

"Have you any idea of the things I had to do to get it?" asked Harvey.

"Yes, I do. I found the bodies, remember?"

"You found some of the bodies, Melody. And yeah, I do love that house. I dreamed about it for years. I just wish I could actually spend some time there to enjoy it."

Keeping her eyes on the road, Melody shuffled in her seat, making herself comfortable for the long drive to London.

"This is the last one, Melody."

"Last what?"

"The last trip. At least for a while. I'm supposed to be retired with my feet up."

"It's Reg's wedding, Harvey. You can't not go. He'd be devastated."

"I know, I know. I'm going, aren't I? But after this, no more. London has a lot of memories for me. Most of them I'd like to leave behind and forget about."

"They can't all be bad."

"No, not all of them. But enough to keep me away. Besides, every time I go there, something happens. I need to keep my head down. Julios would have a fit if he was alive and knew about the things I've done."

"Julios?" said Melody. "Wow, I haven't heard that name for a long time."

"Yeah, well," said Harvey, "it doesn't mean I've forgotten about him. The bloke was like a dad to me."

"Do you ever think about your real dad?" asked Melody, as she pulled out of their lane and onto the main road, a dual carriageway that would link them to the main artery network of French motorways.

"Yeah, of course. But there are no images. Not like Julios. I've got memories of him. As clear as day, most of them."

"What's your favourite?"

"Memory?" asked Harvey. "I don't have a favourite."

"So what one do you remember the most? If I said the name Julios to you, what memory does it invoke?"

"The one of him lying on the ground full of bullet holes."

Melody was silent.

"You asked," said Harvey.

"And I wish I hadn't."

Melody sat for a while, deep in thought and quiet.

"How about you?" asked Harvey.

"Me?" asked Melody. "How about me what?"

"Your favourite memory." He asked the question to break the silence, but waited for the answer, intrigued as to her reply.

"My parents. My dog. No specific memory," said Melody.

"So if I mentioned your parents, what memory does it invoke?"

"The funeral," she replied, then gave him a sideways glance and returned her attention to the road.

"See," said Harvey. "I'm not the only psycho in this car."

"There it is again," said Melody.

"There's what again?"

"That sense of humour," said Melody, as she dropped to third gear, manoeuvred into the outside lane and overtook a lorry. "You should be careful. You might be losing your mean streak."

CHAPTER SEVEN

"See you tomorrow, boss," said Tyler, as he heaved his work bag over his shoulder.

"Are you not coming for a beer, Tyler?" said George. "Come on, son. Dirty Harry had a kid yesterday. We're going to wet the baby's head."

"Not tonight, George. Sorry, mate."

"Tyler, what is it? Don't you like us? Is Frank too hard on you? Don't worry about him. Look at the bleeding size of you. You could knock him over with your little finger." George slammed the door to his van and moved around it to stand beside Tyler.

"No, George, I've got training, that's all, and I need to check on my mum. Another time, yeah?"

"When? Christmas?" said George. "That's a long way off, Tyler. Are you okay, mate?" George lowered his voice. "Are you alright for cash, son? Do you need a bit more work?"

"No, it's fine, George. Honest."

"I can get you on the tools if you want. We'll start you off slow. No more fetching bricks and muck for us lot. You'll have your own labourer."

"No, seriously," said Tyler. He backed away from George. "I'm fine, mate. Honest. I like the graft. It keeps me in shape."

"Yeah, but you can get some serious cash on the tools. Price work, Tyler. That's where the money is."

"Yeah, maybe one day. Listen, I'm running late. I've got to see my mum and get to the gym."

"Alright, son, if you're sure. But listen, if there's something you need, you tell me. Alright?"

"Yeah, no worries," said Tyler, as he moved towards the gate of the construction site. He turned and called back to George. "Hey, George."

"What's up?" said George, as he opened his van door, leaned in and started the engine.

"Thanks," said Tyler. "I'll have a think about getting on the tools."

"You do that, son," said George, and he climbed into his van.

Tyler turned right out of the site, tightened his hooded sweatshirt around his neck, and pulled on his beanie hat. He worked himself into a stride that was just out of his comfort zone, enough to raise his heart rate, but not too much to tire him out on the three-mile walk home.

The winter sky loomed above, dark and foreboding, and although the rain had stopped, the roads still held their sheen, magnifying the lights of passing cars and street lights. Tyler turned onto Commercial Road. It was the easiest route home and a straight line from Poplar to Shadwell. There were faster routes to take, but they meant entering the maze of back streets. The direct route gave Tyler a chance to go over the things that the old man had told him the night before. Lloyd had advised him to listen to the old man; the last thing Tyler wanted to do was make him repeat himself. He needed to prove how good he was and demonstrate his potential.

He opened the front door to find his mum standing in the kitchen. She was stirring a saucepan of soup and beamed at him as he closed the door.

"You're up and about," said Tyler. "Shouldn't you be resting?"

"Oh, Tyler, I can't lie in bed all day. I get up when I can. Anyway, how was your day, love? Do you want some soup?"

"Here, let me, Mum. Why don't you sit down? I'll bring it through to you."

"Stop fussing. It's only soup. I can manage," she replied. "So? How was your day then? Tell me about the world outside these four walls."

"You're better off inside, Mum. It rained all day."

"Yeah, I know. I heard it on the window. And the wind. I hope you wrap up warm at work."

"Of course, Mum. It's hard work though, up and down ladders. I'm usually stripped down to my t-shirt within twenty minutes."

"Does George make you work in the rain?"

"We all work in the rain, Mum, or else we don't get paid. We do the internal walls when it's wet outside. You can't lay a wet brick, Mum." He talked to his mum from his room as he changed into his gym shorts, a fresh t-shirt and clean socks.

"Are you training tonight?" she asked.

"Yeah," said Tyler, as he pulled the door closed to his bedroom. "The old man's giving me some of his time. Lloyd said I should make the most of it. I reckon I can really show them what I can do, Mum. Now could be the chance I've been waiting for."

"Which one's Lloyd?" his mum asked.

"He helps the old man. He's a really nice bloke. Knows his stuff too."

"Will you be late?"

"I don't know, Mum. If the old man wants to carry on, I'd be stupid not to."

"Oh," she replied, "okay, dear. I don't want to stop you doing what you want to do." Her tone had dropped. The cheerful demeanour had all but gone.

"Why don't we do something special this weekend, Mum? If you're feeling up to it?"

"Yeah. Why not, love?" she replied with a smile as she turned the gas off. "Maybe I'll cook a roast dinner. You'll need to go shopping though."

Tyler picked up his bag and slung it over his shoulder, then stepped into the kitchen to kiss his mum goodbye. But as he did, the saucepan she was using to pour soup slipped in her hand. The hot broth splashed onto the counter, causing his mum to step back in alarm. Her foot kicked a chair, but before she fell, Tyler reached in, pulled the pan from her hands, put his arm around his mum to steady her, and then set the pan down on the stove.

He switched off the gas and wiped the mess.

"It's alright," he said. "You only spilt a bit of it. There's loads left."

"I'm sorry, Tyler, I-"

"Hey," he said, rubbing her arm, "go in the living room and sit down. I'll bring this in for you."

He poured the soup into a bowl and fetched a spoon from the drawer, marvelling at the fact that they didn't have a nice TV, the curtains needed replacing and the carpets needed burning, but they had soup spoons in the cutlery drawer like a fancy restaurant.

Tyler glanced out of the window to the street below. There were no tell-tale signs of exhaust smoke in the cold night air. No interior lights were on in any of the parked cars. But he couldn't shake the feeling that it wouldn't be the last he saw of the two men.

His mum was sat at a little four-seater table by the window in the living room. Tyler set down the bowl and flicked on the TV. He placed the remote beside his mum and gave her a kiss on the cheek.

"Leave all this here when you're done," he said. "I'll clean up when I get back."

"I'm sorry, Tyler," she said.

"What're you sorry for?"

"I'm getting more useless by the day."

The statement saddened Tyler but he couldn't let his mum see. He coughed to clear his throat and then stepped across the room to put his arm around her.

"Your job is to love me, right?" he said. "And my job is to look after you." He looked around the room. It wasn't much but it was clean and tidy. "I think we're doing alright, Mum."

He kissed the top of her head and returned to the front door, giving her a wave as he pulled it closed behind him. Then he took the single flight of stairs to the ground floor two at a time.

A biting wind found his neck and ears as soon as he left the building. He pulled on his beanie hat and wrapped his hooded sweatshirt closer around his neck, then found his pace and got into the rhythm, working through combinations in his head as he walked.

A group of teenagers huddled together outside a block of flats. The smell of weed was thick even in the strong, cool wind. They quietened as he approached. All four heads turned to watch him. Tyler didn't turn away. He kept looking ahead with his fists clenched inside the pockets of his hoodie.

No abuse or taunts came his way, so Tyler kept moving. He'd done well to get through school and avoid much of the trouble. His grades hadn't been great, and aside from one close call with the police, his record was clean. Many kids his age left school on the back foot with records for stealing or abuse or some kind of drugs possession. But Tyler had steered clear, finding solace in the various gyms he frequented. Even the single infraction he'd had with the law had been instigated by others seeing how far they could push him until he snapped.

It was because of his size; he knew it was. But they were soon sorry.

They wouldn't be pushing anybody else around in a hurry. But Tyler would do whatever it took to avoid any more trouble. The policewoman who had spoken to him had been nice. It was as if she'd understood and saw that Tyler was a nice guy deep down. He remembered how she'd sat on the blue plastic mattress in his cell, while Tyler buried his face in his hands. His mind often recalled the memory. Someone on TV had once said that certain events were turning points in life, and that by recognising them, no matter how painful it is, the stronger the lesson will be. At the time, Tyler hadn't even realised how hard he'd hit the boy. He hadn't known the damage he'd caused. It was a blur. But when the officer who sat beside Tyler told him the boy was no longer in critical condition, it was as if something inside Tyler snapped. The very thing that held him upright and gave strength to his bones was gone.

He'd crumpled to a heap on the sticky, blue, plastic mattress and the tears had flowed.

The smell hit him as soon as he opened the door to the gym, causing memories of the police officer and the blue mattress to fade away. It was a close second to smelling his mum's roast dinner from outside the flat. Nothing would ever beat that smell.

"Alright, Lloyd?" said Tyler, as he dumped his bag on a bench to change his shoes.

"All good," said Lloyd. His baritone voice lay beneath the dull thumps of punch bags and muffled voices from outside the changing room. He waited for Tyler to change his shoes so he could wrap his hands. "Do you work outside?"

"Yeah, labouring for a brickie. We're on a job in Limehouse at the minute. It's not too far. What about you? Do you do anything else?"

"Anything other than getting this lot gloved up?" said Lloyd. "No. I'm too old for much else now."

"As long as you're happy, I guess," said Tyler, holding out his right hand.

"The old man's in a good mood today. Do what he says when he says."

"Yeah, right," said Tyler. "Do you think he'll put me up for a fight soon?"

Lloyd pulled the wrap tight and held Tyler's glove open for him to slide his hand inside.

"Be patient."

Tyler nodded.

Once Lloyd had wrapped and gloved his left hand, Tyler emerged from the changing room in the gym. Two punch bags swung back and forth as two young boys practised jabs and staying on their toes.

"That's good, boys," said Lloyd. "Look light on your feet, Billy. Don't settle."

"I remember all that," said Tyler. "I used to look up to the kids like me thinking they must know it all."

"Nothing changes, Tyler. I've been in this game for forty years and nothing changes but the names and faces. You know that smell you like?"

"The smell of hard work?" said Tyler.

"It smelled the same back then too, just a different name and a different face. Get warmed up on the bags, Tyler. The old man will be with you soon."

Tyler moved his body from side to side as he walked through the centre of the gym, running through combinations in the air. He rolled his neck, waiting for the click of his joints, then threw a few light jabs at the bag.

A breath of fresh, cold air licked at his bare legs, enough for him to turn to see who had opened the door.

Two men, both huge, walked in and let the door close behind them. The first man wore a long, dark, double-breasted jacket, as if he was a city worker, but with smart jeans, a casual shirt and brown leather boots. The second man wore a short bomber jacket, light blue jeans and smart shoes.

The pair looked comfortable in the gym, not intimidated as some people look when they walk in for the first time. They eyed the boys on the bags, and then the teenager that the old man was training in the ring. Then they found Tyler at the far end of the room. Tyler nodded then continued with his jabs, feeling the stretch of his muscles with each punch.

The two men both sat on the small bench beside the door. The smartest of the pair played with his phone. The other watched the old man. But every now and then, Tyler would glance across to find one of them staring at him. Just like they had the night before.

"Tyler, you're up," called the old man.

Lloyd held the ropes for the teenager in the ring to climb out. The boy's arms hung by his sides like lead weights. Tyler smiled. He knew the feeling all too well. It was a feeling that didn't go away the more training he did; it just took longer to tire.

"Let's go," said the old man.

Then he eyed the two men on the bench. They made eye contact but neither spoke.

"You remember what we did yesterday?" asked the old man, slipping back into the pads as Tyler ducked beneath ropes.

"Jab, jab, hook?" said Tyler, punching the air with the combination.

"Not the moves, Tyler," said the old man. "The eyes and the feet. Look at my eyes, watch for my feet, and roll with the punches. Let's go. Right, left, right."

Tyler threw the first punch before the old man had finished, but he was ready with the pad.

"Good, Tyler." The old man sidestepped as Tyler threw the hook, which missed. "Come on. Dance with me. Get me on the ropes, Tyler."

The old man moved around faster than he looked capable of moving. The two men stared up at Tyler as he jabbed at the pads. But Tyler's punches were weak, his feet were flat, and the old man moved before he'd finished one combo.

"Tyler, look at me. Let's go. You think I'm dancing for my health?"

Tyler bounced into action, and let three punches go in quick succession.

"That's better. Again. Watch my feet. Watch my feet."

The old man's footwork changed. His leading arm switched to his left, so Tyler adjusted the combo to left, right, left, and powered them into the pads.

"On your toes, Tyler."

No matter how hard he tried, Tyler couldn't shake the stares of the two men at the door. He threw one punch and the old man shifted the pad to the right then returned the blow to Tyler's head.

"Wake up, Tyler. Let's go." He offered the pads again but caught Tyler's glance at the men by the door.

"Right. Stop," said the old man. He shook the pads from his hands, turned, and leaned on the ropes.

"Can I help you, boys?" he asked. His authority in the gym quietened the thuds of gloves on bags and skip ropes until all eyes were on him. "I said, can I help you, boys?"

The larger of the two men stood up, followed by his counterpart. Lloyd walked over to them, bridging the gap. He spoke in a quiet voice so as not to antagonise the men. But his deep grumble could be heard by all.

"Are you waiting for anyone?" asked Lloyd.

The bigger of the two men looked as though he was about to say something, but then closed his mouth.

"Can I politely ask you both to leave?" said Lloyd. "We don't want trouble, but the boys need to train."

The lead man shook his head, gestured for his friend to follow, and they left the building.

"Right, the show is over," said the old man to the room. "Let me hear those bags going."

The old man turned back to Tyler.

"Friends of yours?" he asked.

"Never seen them before."

Tyler threw two jabs and a hook at the old man, who blocked them with the pads and returned to his dance around the ring.

CHAPTER EIGHT

The Golden Ring Pub was a Victorian building with heavy brick-work and large windows. It was split into two bars. The first was a saloon with a long bar across the back wall and booths around the edges. There was a small stage area at the front where the land-lord hosted a jam night every Thursday evening. A well-reputed local band would play a few hits from the sixties or seventies, mainly classic rock, and then other people could join them. Guitarists, singers, drummers and bass players, mostly bedroom musicians, took the opportunity to get in front of a crowd to perform. It was one thing to play a song note for note in the confines of your own home, but to perform it in front of a crowd was a different game.

The jam night brought in customers from all over the East End. The host band, Double Trouble, was comprised of middle-aged men who had each mastered their instruments but never made the big time. That didn't stop them rocking the Golden Ring for one night a week and showing the wannabes how it was done.

They opened with a Gary Moore number, Still Got The Blues For You, a steady beat to warm up to with enough of a solo for the guitarist to stretch his fingers. The crowd loved it, and the noise from the saloon raised a notch.

It was for this reason that John Cooper chose to sit in the other half of the pub on Thursdays, the family side. It was decorated with exactly the same red-patterned carpet and textured wallpaper as the saloon, with the same oak bar, but without the screaming Marshall amps and Les Paul guitars or an eight-piece Ludwig drum kit being thrashed by a six-foot pipe-fitter.

John had a wing-back seat beside the large fireplace. It was where he sat every Thursday night. From there, he could see the rest of the pub, whoever entered through the doors, and he had the benefit of having his back to the window.

The family side wasn't busy. Most of the clientele were watching the band perform, so John enjoyed having the place to himself. Two youngsters were playing pool, but they were local boys, probably just turned eighteen, and they knew to keep the noise down. Keeping a few local boys on his side was something he'd always done, and he found the practice worked well. He'd explained his thought process to Mick once when they'd both been sat in that very spot.

"Society works in layers, Mick. Although you might think you've got your ear to the ground, you only know what's going on in the layer in which you reside."

"What, like a sandwich, John? Is that what you're saying?"

"If that's the analogy that works for you, then yeah, Mick. Like a sandwich. A triple-decker club sandwich. The top layer is where the mayo and lettuce is. That's where the politicians are, the top cops, and all the stuffy businessmen who go home to their vanilla wives every night, pleased with their day's work but absolutely ignorant to the rest of society. You see, those in the top layer still have two more layers beneath them, even three sometimes. They might have an inkling of what happens in the layer below, but the next layer? No. They don't have a clue, Mick. Blind to it, they are."

"I get you. So who's in the bottom layer?"

"The bottom layer, Mick, is the one that gets crushed by the weight of the layers above. That's where the tomatoes go. We're talking street gangs, drug dealers, thieves and the lowest rung of society. In the same way that the top brass doesn't have a clue what goes on in the bottom layer of the sandwich, the bottom layer has no clue what goes on in the top of the sandwich. That's why there's so much disconnect in society. The local government makes changes that they think is going to solve a problem and all it does is create new problems, different ones, in the bottom layer. And the cycle starts over."

"So where are we then?" asked Mick.

"We, Mick, are the meat. Crispy bacon and turkey stuffing. We reside in the middle layer. We are neither blind to the tomatoes nor blind to the mayo and salad on top. The trouble is, Mick, in most restaurants, you don't get much meat in a club sandwich. They stuff it with tomatoes and mayo and lettuce when all we really want is meat. The good stuff. In fact, without the crispy bacon and turkey, the lettuce and mayo would be nothing. And likewise for the tomatoes. Nobody needs a tomato on its own, Mick, do they?"

"No, John."

"So we sit strategically in the middle. Of course, we know some lettuces and we use them to understand what's happening above because that's how we don't get caught doing what we do. Right?"

"Right, John."

"And we know a few tomatoes too because that's how we know what's going on below."

"I understand."

"But we need to have some tomatoes on our side, Mick. And we need to have some lettuce watching our backs too. There's far too many tomatoes in this sandwich that need to be controlled. Just as the mayo has far too much power; it needs to be culled every now and then. That's why we have local elections."

Mick looked a little lost.

"See those two boys playing pool?" asked John.

Mick nodded.

"I could quite easily turf them out for being underage. But what's that going to do?"

"I don't know, John."

"Well, they'll come back tonight, when we're all at home, and they'll smash the bleeding windows, won't they? They might even start a little fire that gets out of control. You remember being a kid, right?"

"Right," said Mick.

"So by having a few tomatoes on our side, by keeping them keen, then firstly, we don't get our windows broke or the place burned down, and secondly, we send them in like little soldier tomatoes and pay them a bit of pocket money for any information they feed back to us. It keeps them sweet."

"The same way we pay off the top brass?"

"Exactly, Mick. You see? Being in the middle layer is a great place to be."

"Right," said Mick, and sat back in his chair.

John could see the analogy had blown his mind.

John's phone buzzed on the table and snapped him from his memory.

"Mick," he said, dismissing the greeting, "give me some good news."

"We've got someone for you to talk to. Where shall we bring him?"

"You said you had two options. Is this option one or option two?"

"This is option one, John."

"I'm in the boozer, Mick. Bring him here."

CHAPTER NINE

The lights of London lit the horizon like a distant, hazy, orange dome as Melody and Harvey made their way along the M2 from Dover. During one of the fuel stops, they had pulled the roof back up on the little sports car. As they'd made their way through France, the heater had been turned on, and less than one hundred miles from Reg's house in South London, the temperature was raised another notch. Harvey had removed his jacket and relished the cool breeze that found a gap in the old car's soft top. Melody had kept her jacket on and warmed her hands in the heated air that was pumped through the dashboard vent.

After a fifteen-and-a-half-hour journey, with three stops for fuel, bathroom and food, Melody parked the car in a bay reserved for visitors outside Reg and Jess' flat in Clapham. The engine shuddered to a stop beside a new Volkswagen camper van and Melody sat back in her seat.

"I'm beat," she said.

"You did well," said Harvey, opening the door and stretching his back and neck.

Melody followed suit as Harvey pulled their bags from the rear seat. A clatter of paws on the tarmac stopped him, and he turned to find his old dog, Boon, tearing across the little car park with his ears flat against his head. Boon slammed into Melody with excitement, ran a few rings around her then settled for her to stroke and dote on him. Then he was off again. He bounced around the car, saw Harvey, then came to a sudden stop. He sat straight like a soldier on parade, looking up at his old master with his tail banging against the ground, as he waited for Harvey's acknowledgement.

Harvey stared him in the eyes and waited a few seconds. The dog was bursting to be welcomed, his front legs twitching with restraint.

"Good boy," said Harvey.

The dog remained still but his tail beat harder.

"Come," said Harvey, and the dog erupted into a frenzy of running rings and nosing Harvey's hand for affection.

"Be careful. He's a trained killer," said a familiar voice. "You'd better watch out."

Harvey straightened and found Reg standing beside Melody on the other side of the car with a smile on his face from ear to ear.

"The dog, I mean," continued Reg. Then he put his arms around Melody and gave her a hug.

Harvey shooed Boon away, grabbed the last bag from the car, and then slammed the door. Reg had walked around the car and Harvey offered him his hand to shake, but Reg pulled him in for a hug, which raised a smile on Melody's face.

"Good to see you, Harvey," said Reg, giving him a last squeeze before letting go.

"Likewise, Reg," said Harvey. "Is Jess inside?"

"She's just had to pop to the office. She'll be back in a few minutes. What do you think of the new van?"

"The camper?" said Melody. "Is that yours?"

"Just got it," replied Reg. "Fully kitted out with beds, a cooker and all the technology I could fit inside."

"So it's a mobile criminal investigation unit?" said Melody. "I thought you'd left all that behind?"

"Ah, well, you can take the nerd out of the crime, Melody, but you can't take the crime out of the nerd. Come on, let's get you guys inside. How was the drive? You must be shattered."

"It wasn't too bad," said Melody. "But I am glad it's over."

Reg's flat was on the first floor of a small but expensive-looking block of two-story-high private flats. Well-maintained lawns encircled the building with two pathways that cut through the grass and a new iron fence that ran the perimeter of the complex.

"This is nice," said Melody, as Reg held the front door open for them to pass through.

"Thanks. We thought we deserved an upgrade when I got the new job."

After stepping inside, Reg poured Melody a glass of wine, then handed Harvey a bottle of water.

"So how about a tour?" asked Melody.

"A tour? Well, what you see is what you get really. You're standing in the kitchen-diner. The lounge is behind you and your bedroom is through the door at the end. Our bedroom is over here. Both of them are en-suite and there's a small washroom in the hallway."

"It's great, Reg," said Harvey. "Thanks for putting us up."

"No, thank you for coming to our wedding. Without you, I'd have exactly one guest on my side, and he's got bad breath and too much hair," said Reg, looking at Boon who sat by Harvey's feet staring up at him.

"And how has Boon been? Are you guys still happy with him?" asked Melody.

"He's great. Jess adores him. She wouldn't let you take him if you tried."

"I think he's happier here with you, Reg," said Harvey. He put his hand on the dog's head and ran his fingers along his snout. "I couldn't give him the time he deserves."

"So how's the new job going?" asked Melody. She sat down in

one of the comfy leather armchairs and rested her wine glass on her knee.

"It's good," said Reg. "I haven't been shot at, blown up or kidnapped, and I haven't had to break any laws or risk imprisonment of any kind."

"Sounds dull," said Harvey, sitting on the armchair opposite Melody. Boon followed and sat beside him so that Harvey could continue stroking his head.

"I'm head of the research department, so I have a few other people in my team and they're all great. Quiet. No fuss. Plus the pay is a lot better and I haven't had to sign the official secrets act. I should have done it years ago."

"No," said Melody, "you'd have missed all the fun we had, and besides, you wouldn't have met Jess."

At the mention of her name, the front door opened and Jess walked in. She didn't bother to close the door. Instead, she ran to Melody and gave her a big hug. Then she approached Harvey and wrapped her arms around him.

"Wow, two hugs in twenty minutes," said Melody. "That must be a record for Harvey."

"It's great to see you two," said Jess, her public school, middle-class accent shining through. "I bet Boon was pleased to see you both."

Boon's head flinched at his name, but he made no effort to move away from Harvey.

"Did you get it?" asked Reg. He raised his eyebrows at Jess, who was pouring herself a glass of wine. She stepped across the room and topped up Melody's glass.

"I did," she said, and pulled a folded piece of paper from her pocket. She handed it to Reg.

"So, Harvey," Reg began, "Melody messaged me a few hours ago with an idea."

Harvey stopped stroking Boon and sat upright in the chair, causing the dog to nuzzle his hand for more attention.

"Jess has been to the office and done some digging around, and well, we thought you might like this."

Reg handed Harvey the folded piece of paper and stepped back.

"What is it?" asked Harvey as he unfolded it.

But he soon saw for himself.

"Is this Julios?" asked Harvey in disbelief.

"Only his family know his whereabouts," said Jess. "I had to pull some strings, but, well, we thought you'd like to visit."

CHAPTER TEN

"Good, Tyler. Get yourself washed up," said the old man as he shook the pads from his hands. "You listened and you've got good energy. Keep that up."

Lloyd leaned over the ropes and untied Tyler's gloves, then began to unravel the wrap. Tyler's right hand was unwrapped first. He loved the tingling sensation as his skin breathed the air after being constrained for so long.

"Your posture is improving. Can you feel it in your back?" asked Lloyd.

It was only once Lloyd had mentioned it that Tyler realised his lower back wasn't aching as much as it had in the past. He rubbed his hand across his back as Lloyd unwrapped his left hand.

"I told you. You need to listen to him. Your feet were faster too," said Lloyd.

"I didn't notice that," replied Tyler.

"That's because you were paying attention. But I saw it well enough."

Lloyd pulled the last of the wrap free then held the ropes open for Tyler to slip through.

"Thanks, Lloyd," said Tyler, as he dropped to the floor.

He picked up his bag and scanned the room for the old man. But he was nowhere to be seen. So Tyler walked past the three punch bags and into the changing room. The old man slammed the door on an old washing machine full of towels, span the dial and hit the power button.

"I just wanted to say thanks," said Tyler. "For staying and helping me. I appreciate the extra time."

"We all need a leg up every now and then," the old man replied without looking at Tyler.

He carried on cleaning the little changing room while he spoke. "You did good. I mean it. But you need to be consistent. You've got a punch like a mule and when you're focused, you're a good boxer. But you need to curb those emotions. They're your weakness. Show your opponent that and you'll spend more time on your back than those hookers on the street."

"I'm not emotional," said Tyler. But he heard his tone turn defensive.

The old man cast him a sideways glance, then continued to wash the shower down with water and squeegee the tiled wall.

"I'll work on it," said Tyler.

"Good. You do that."

"So when do you think I'll be ready?" asked Tyler.

"Ready for what?"

"To fight. When do you think I can get in the ring?"

"You were in the ring tonight, son. Or was you concentrating so hard you missed it?" The old man smiled to himself.

"You know what I mean. I want to fight. Maybe if I had a target to train for-"

"You'll go up against some other dam fool when I say you're ready. Until then, you're just a very big rock that needs a hell of a lot of polishing."

"But how do you know I'm not ready?" asked Tyler.

The old man stood straight, switched off the water and tossed the squeegee into a bucket. He pulled a towel from the slatted wooden bench and dried his hands, then leaned on the washing machine.

He eyed Tyler and sucked at his teeth as if he was choosing his words carefully.

"How many boys out there tonight, son?" the old man asked.

Tyler glanced into the gym but saw only Lloyd pushing around the broom.

"No-one," he replied.

"No-one," repeated the old man. "And what time is it?"

Tyler looked up at the cheap plastic clock on the wall that showed only the twelve, three, six and nine, but had a picture of Frank Bruno's face on it.

"Eleven thirty," said Tyler.

"So do you think I stay here late at night to train you for free for my health? Is that what you think?"

"No, I-"

"I'm giving you years of experience because I believe in you, Tyler. Someone like you could go far. You have the power. You have the dedication. But you need to calm those emotions down. They're your crux. When you show me you can stay in control, I'll think about putting you in the ring with someone other than me or Lloyd."

"Right," said Tyler.

"Don't be disheartened, son. Your time will come. But most importantly, don't let me down."

"I won't, I-"

"If you want to fight in a ring, if you want to have a few hundred people all watch you get your nose smashed flat and your eyes blackened, then be my guest. Join some other gym with some other trainer. But if you want to go places, son, you stick with me. You work hard and you damn well listen."

"I will," said Tyler.

"Who were those two men?" asked the old man.

The positive feedback from the old man and Lloyd had overshadowed the two men who had sat on the bench in the gym earlier that evening.

Tyler shook his head. "I don't know."

But the old man had an air of disbelief. Tyler could see it in the way he threw a shower gel bottle into the little cupboard above the sink, then slammed the door.

"Honest," said Tyler. "I haven't seen them before."

The old man dropped a full black bag outside the changing room, rinsed his hands and dried them on one of the fresh towels he'd piled on the towel rack. He leaned on the door frame.

"If you train with me, you fight with me. Nobody else," said the old man, supporting his statement with a shake of his head. "I'm not spending my evenings training you for some other toe-rag to get you beaten to a pulp. I'm too long in the tooth for all that. Been there. Seen that. Bought the t-shirt."

"Yeah, I know," said Tyler. "Why would I fight for anyone else?"

"Those two men," said the old man, "they're trouble. I can smell it a mile away. If they approach you, I want to know. You can talk to me or Lloyd. And don't think that because I'm old, I don't know people. There isn't one person in this game that I've never heard of. There isn't anyone worth their salt who don't know me. I can tell you this, son. There's some nasty pieces of work out there who prey on kids like you. You come to me, I'll help. But if you go against me, Tyler, you'll make an enemy you wish you hadn't. And trust me, in this game, an enemy is the last thing you need."

"Understood. And thanks again for trusting me. For putting your faith in me."

"Just don't let me down, son," said the old man. "Now scat. I thought you had a sick mum to look after?"

Tyler pushed off the wall and edged around the old man. "See you tomorrow, yeah?"

"Yep. Same time. Same place," said the old man. "Oh, and son?"

Tyler turned in the doorway, his eyebrows raised in anticipation of more words of wisdom from the old man.

"The next time you see an old man cleaning up after a load of young kids, emptying bins and washing towels, do yourself a favour and get stuck in." He offered Tyler a friendly smile. "Go on. Get out of here. We've all got homes to go to."

CHAPTER ELEVEN

A breath of fresh air licked at John Cooper's feet as Jack entered the family side of the pub and held the door open. A stranger walked in. He was cautious and checked either side of him before committing to the room. Mick followed, nodded at John and led the stranger towards the fireplace, while Jack closed and guarded the door.

John remained seated but offered his hand to the young man.

"What's your name, son?" he asked mid-shake.

"Blake," the big man replied.

"Is it just Blake? Or do you have a last name like the rest of us?"

"Green," came the reply.

"Blake Green?" said John, sitting back in his seat and crossing his legs. "Well, Blake Green, why don't you take a seat? Can I get you a drink?"

Blake shook his head.

"Mick, get him a drink, will you? He looks like he needs loosening up."

"I don't drink," said Blake.

Mick raised his eyebrow at John who nodded once.

"Just water, Mick."

"I don't want a water either."

Mick walked behind the bar and poured two brandies for John and himself, and pulled a bottle of sparkling water from the fridge for Blake.

"Tell me, Blake," said John. "What does a man your size have to eat every day to stay that big?"

"Are you going to tell me what this is all about?" said Blake. His tone cut straight through the niceties that John had laid out. "Tell me why I'm here. I don't know you, or your two mates, so tell me what the bleeding hell is going on and I might be able to help you."

"I bet it's eggs," said John. "Eggs and chicken. Am I right?"

"What are you talking about?" said Blake. "Eggs and chicken?"

"And rice. I forgot rice. They all eat rice apparently."

"Who do? Who eats rice, chicken and eggs?"

"You do," said John. "All fighters your size eat rice, chicken and eggs. Do you enjoy fighting, Blake?"

"Listen, mate. Who are you? And why am I here?"

"Mick tells me you're a bailiff. Is that right?" asked John, ignoring Blake's question but enjoying his growing impatience. "You're a debt collector. Is that right?"

"So what if I am?"

"I bet a man like you collects quite a few debts, don't you? I imagine when some low life scumbag opens his front door and sees you on his doorstep, he must drop his lunch. What do you reckon, Mick?"

"I reckon you're right, John," said Mick. "I reckon they hand over everything they own when they see this fellow standing on their doorstep, especially in that lovely leather jacket."

"I don't know who you are, and honestly, I don't care. I need to go," said Blake.

"Do many of them put up a fight, Blake?" asked John. "You know, the offending parties, as it were."

"Some. It's mostly the women that give me the most grief because they know a bloke won't hit them back."

"Ah, most blokes wouldn't. But some men would, and they do, Blakey," said John. "What type are you?"

"What? What do you mean what type am I?" said Blake. "I wouldn't hit a woman ever."

"What if someone paid you?" asked John.

"No, mate. The answer is still no. It's not right."

"Do you think that some women deserve to be hit by a man, Blake?"

Blake paused. It was the answer John was looking for.

"I take it by the pause that yes, you do think some women deserve to be hit by a man."

Blake began to protest, but John held his hand out to quieten him. Controlling the conversation was key to getting the answers he wanted without asking the question that Blake didn't want to hear.

"It's okay. I agree. I've met a few in my time that could have done with being dragged into an alley and taught a lesson. You see, Blake, some women, as you rightly said, prey on men because they know they won't hit them back. It's cowardly, that's what that is. But you know what? Sometimes, just one or two need to be taught a lesson. It's a form of bullying, you know?" said John. "Did you know that a third of all domestic abuse victims in Britain are male?"

"This is a joke," said Blake. "You have about three seconds to explain what's going on before I walk out."

John took his drink from Mick and watched as the water was placed on the table in front of Blake. He checked his watch to make sure the three seconds were up.

"So?" said John.

"So what?"

"The three seconds are up and I haven't explained what's going on," said John. He slipped his tumbler onto the table and sat back, interlacing his fingers and letting his chin rest on his knuckles. "Have you always been so emotional, Blake?"

"I don't need this," said Blake. He pushed himself out of the chair. "I don't play games, mate. I don't have time for them."

"Jack," called John, as Blake shoved his chair back, "stand aside, will you, and let young Blakey out."

Jack did as requested, and John watched as Blake's hand grabbed the door handle and pulled the cold air into the room once more.

"Oh, one more thing, Blake," he said, taking another sip of his brandy. "Before you go."

The big man turned to face John with the dark, wet night waiting behind his huge frame that filled the doorway. John nodded at Mick who pulled a single photograph from his pocket and handed it to him.

"Your little girl," said John, studying the photograph. He waited until he had Blake's attention and saw the big man moving towards him in his peripheral vision. "She's very pretty. She's the image of her mum, isn't she?"

CHAPTER TWELVE

A blanket of leaves lay on the damp ground in chronological layers of death. Fresh leaves crunched under Harvey's boot, while older generations that had been exposed to the wet turned to pulp and became an unidentifiable part of the environment.

Rows of headstones stood upright like proud sentries guarding their posts while below them, the cycle of life and death rolled on. The deterioration of the leaves on the surface, the unending quarrel of insects below, and below them, the bodies of the dead in their long journey of decay, as piece by piece, their bodies returned to the earth.

The East London Crematorium and Cemetery spanned thirteen acres of hallowed ground. It was a pride of green, a walled-in escape from industry, evolution and the chaos of city life, a pocket of peace for those who rested.

An avenue of trees greeted Harvey along with the calm aura of eternal rest. Beyond the avenue, shrouded by oaks and elms, was the chapel and to the sides of the avenue lay the dead. Some of the headstones had fallen with age. The dark and crumbled stone had cracked or broken. But some fresh graves shone bright white with the gaiety of a freshman, naive to the realm of eternal peace. Slowly, they would too fade and succumb to the cycle of life, as day by day, week by week, and year by year, they perished, as do all things.

Standing tall among the older graves, adorned with great Celtic crosses, the faded, once-cherished names of the dead stood between carved angels, saints and the ever-present Jesus, nailed to a cross, a symbol of sacrifice.

The grave of Julios Saville was not guarded by an angel reaching for the heavens, nor was Harvey's mentor's journey to the afterlife accompanied by an ornate saint, carved in granite by the loving hands of a mason. Instead, a simple plaque, seven inches squared, was fixed to a lump of marble and set in the earth beside identical markers with identical plaques.

It was a government burial ground offering the minimal contribution of memory to lives who, in the eyes of society, deserved less. Although the simple markers were uniform, Julios' grave was unique. Neighbouring graves were overrun with weeds, seeking a place to hold onto and fighting for light to thrive among the memories, and hide the names of the shunned from the honour of the dead. But Julios' grave was clear as if somebody had pulled the imposing weeds from the earth and exposed his name for all to see. It was the work of pride.

No flowers lay across the bare earth, but the contrast of dark soil against the neighbouring battle of plant life honoured Julios' simple and clutter-free life.

In all the years Harvey had known Julios, his mentor had never once shown an affection for possessions. The cars he drove were simple and cheap. The clothes he wore were bland and nondescript. Not once had Harvey ever visited Julios' home. But he'd imagined it hundreds of times as a basic one-room apartment with an armchair, a bed, perhaps a table, and a landlord willing to ask no questions in return for a monthly cash payment.

On his walk through the graveyard, Harvey had tried to picture what the grave might look like. He'd expected nothing grand, knowing that a state burial would offer the minimum viable option.

But what had been clear in Harvey's mind had been the name. In his mind's eye, the carved letters portrayed finality and reflected the greatness of the man Harvey had admired and looked up to more than anybody else during his childhood.

But the stark reality hit him hard. The small chunk of synthetic marble with a template plaque punched out in some factory by a cold-hearted machine to form the words 'Julios Saville' and the date of his death offered no sense of the person.

It had been Julios who had trained Harvey to be the man he'd become. Stealth, defence, and attack were at the core of those lessons, as was the power of barely existing until it was time to strike. But when he did strike, he was taught the ability to read an opponent before either man made a move, which added weight to the perfection in every placement of his feet and accuracy in every delivery of a blow. Julios Saville was a dangerous man to stand toe to toe with, and over years of training, Harvey had taken those skills, and added his own blend of prolonged suffering.

Defence and attack were not the only attributes Harvey had gleaned from his mentor. Their work required a state of mind, and a clean life free of the complexities that the average man collated. There could be no routine for anyone to follow. There could be no item out of place. And there could be no emotion.

But it had been emotion that killed Julios in the end. Harvey thought back to the time when he'd found Julios in the mud, his huge face torn apart by the wheels of a Range Rover. His body riddled with bullet holes. It hadn't been Julios' emotion that killed him, it had been Harvey's. He'd added complexities to what was a very simple job, and it had gone wrong. In the blink of an eye, Julios had been torn from Harvey's life.

Ironically, as Harvey stared down at the pressed plaque and Julios' name, emotions stirred somewhere deep inside. It triggered some hidden part of him that barely existed save for two people: Melody and Julios.

A single tear formed in the corner of Harvey's eye. But as it did, a shape, out of place among the surrounding green, moved at the edge of Harvey's vision.

He glanced up but saw no movement. A trick of the tear?

With a final look at the only evidence that Julios Saville ever existed, Harvey whispered his name. He wasn't sure why. Perhaps it was to substantiate the synthetic block and pressed plaque. Perhaps he was sorry. But Julios would scoff at sorrow. Mostly, thought Harvey, he spoke Julios' name for his own closure. The greatest man he had even known would be remembered in Harvey's heart, as alive as if Julios walked beside him every day, but rarely would his existence ever breach Harvey's lips.

Harvey looked back once more at the plaque, but this time he just nodded at his old friend. Then he walked away. He made his way between two rows of headstones. They were new plots and had retained the glossy sheen of machined marble and granite. It would be years before nature wore down the surfaces to a dull matte finish, and the carved epitaphs would outlive the memories of those who lay beneath them.

At the end of the row, at a crossroads of pathways, all silent, solemn and carpeted with the same broad oak leaves, he glanced back once more at Julios' marker three hundred yards behind him. Bent on one knee and using his hands to clear the earth around Julios' grave was a man. He wore a black jacket and a hat. As if he felt Harvey's stare from afar, he slowly turned his head, and they locked gazes.

Harvey turned to face him. He cocked his head and tried to find some kind of recognition. But the man stood up, glanced back once at Harvey, then took to his heels and ran in the opposite direction.

CHAPTER THIRTEEN

The card reader beeped to unlock the door to the two flats, but it was already open. The lock had been forced. But there was no sign of any other damage. The warm smell of home-baking greeted Tyler when he pushed open the security door on the ground floor. The scent still hung in the air as he sprinted up the single staircase and onto the small landing that split into two entrances, his own flat and his neighbour's flat. He'd recognise the smell of his mum's cooking anywhere. He opened the front door and peered around the frame, unsure of what he'd find.

"You're home late, dear," said his mum from the kitchen.

Tyler closed the door behind him and gave his mum a hug and a kiss.

"Mum, you're up again. What's going on? And you're baking. Mum, you should be resting."

"Oh, leave off," replied his mum. "If I can get up, I will get up. Tomorrow could be my last."

"Don't talk like that."

"Well, don't tell me what to do. Besides, I made some cakes. Your favourite, cherry cupcakes."

"Ah, Mum, I'm training."

"You might be training, Tyler, but you still need food inside you. I haven't seen you eat in god knows how long."

"I eat at work, Mum."

"So you don't want the cakes then?" She glanced across at them on the cooling tray.

"How can I refuse? Thanks, Mum. But seriously, you should be resting. You could have had an accident." Tyler took a cupcake from the tray.

"They'll be hot," his mum warned.

"That's when they're the best," said Tyler with a smile. "Next time you want to get out of bed, can you call me at least?"

"At least what? So you can check up on me?"

"No, Mum. But if I know you're up and about, I can try and get home quicker. It's great you're moving, but you know it only takes one fall. I could even ask Sami next door to pop in and make sure you're okay." He swallowed the remainder of the little cake.

"Well, when you put it like that," she said. Then her face brightened. "How is it?"

Speaking with his mouth full to emphasise the point, Tyler mumbled that the cake was fantastic and gave her two thumbs up, then made his way to his room.

"You didn't tell me where you've been anyway," his mum called from the little kitchen. "You're normally home earlier than this, aren't you? Are you training tonight?"

"Yeah, I'm just getting changed and then I'll go," said Tyler. He walked from his room, pulling a clean t-shirt over his head. "Are you going back to bed? Or shall I get you set up in your chair?"

"Well, I might stay up now I'm awake. I might do some cleaning."

"No, Mum. I've done it all. I did it last night when I got home. Please leave it. Just relax and let me take care of you. Here is your blanket. Here's the TV remote. Do you want a cup of tea before I go?" Tyler held out the blanket, waiting for his mum to sit in her armchair. She walked over slowly. She was frail but far more active than he'd seen her in a long time.

"No tea, dear," she said. "I'll be up and down to the loo all night. Are you going already? Why don't you tell me about your day before you go?"

"Ah, Mum, I'm running late," said Tyler. He threw his bag over his shoulder. "The old man will be waiting for me. But if you're up and about when I get home, we can have a chat then. Okay?"

"Okay, dear. I don't want to stop you doing what you need to do," she said. "I might go back to bed in a while."

"Okay, Mum," said Tyler, and he bent to kiss her on her head.

"That's if I don't get disturbed again."

"What do you mean? Who disturbed you?" said Tyler, his hand holding the door catch.

"Oh, I don't know," his mum replied. "Just two men came knocking."

Tyler remembered the broken door downstairs.

"What did they want?"

"You know, the funny thing is, they never said. I let them in, of course, and offered them a tea. But they were more interested in the photos on the wall."

Behind Tyler, fixed to the hallway wall, were three frames. One was of Tyler and his mum at a family wedding a few years before. Another was of Tyler at his first junior fight. The photo was taken before the bell. It showed Tyler with his gloves on the ropes looking down at his mum taking the picture. A nervous but excited boy. He'd been stocky for his age but had still been just a boy. The third photo was of his dad. A three-quarter-length leather jacket, which was old and worn, hung from his huge shoulders and in his arms was baby Tyler.

"Mum, lock the door behind me and don't let anybody in," said Tyler, and he slammed the door closed.

CHAPTER FOURTEEN

"Is there any news?" said John. He sat back in his office chair and pulled his right foot up onto his left knee. He licked a tissue and wiped a smear from his Oxfords, then tossed the tissue in the bin behind him.

"News, John?" asked Mick.

"News about our new boy Blake. Is he looking good? Is he a winner? Jack, take a seat, mate. You're making the place look untidy," said John. "Sorry, Mick. You were saying?"

"He hasn't lost a fight yet and hasn't seen anything further than round two."

"Knockouts?"

"He's got a punch like a mule, John," said Mick, smiling at the good news.

"But has he got what it takes though, Mick?"

"A few sessions with Jerry, and Blake will be unstoppable, John."

"Good," said John. "Good. That's what I want to hear. When is he meeting Jerry?"

"Tomorrow morning. He'll have the whole day with him."

"And why is he going to do it?" asked John. He left a pause to allow Mick time to consider his answer, then lowered his voice. "What have we got on him? Tell me his weakness."

Mick smiled once more at the opportunity to deliver favourable news.

"He owes money, John. He can't pay his loans."

"So?" said John. "There's a lot of people out there who owe money without the means to pay."

"Most of them are drunks or have gambling habits. Blake has a wife and a young kid and a little bird tells me they might lose their little flat soon, unless they come up with some rent."

A cruel grin spread across John's face, wrinkling his leather-like skin.

"That's the type of news I like to hear, Mick," said John. The news appeased him, and he relaxed back in his chair. "Tell me about our number two. I want him ready too. I want nothing left to chance. Is that clear?"

"Crystal, John," said Mick. "We paid his mum a visit yesterday."

"His mum?" said John. "What was you doing? Asking permission?"

"She's sick. I get the impression she's terminal."

John understood where Mick was going with the conversation.

"And the boy? How does he feel about that?"

"We haven't caught up with him yet. But she's all he's got. The dad died when he was a kid."

"Right," said John. He rested his chin on his steepled fingers and ran the scenarios through in his head. "And he can fight?"

"He's the size of a bleeding house, John. All muscle."

"Who's training him?"

"Old Man McGee in Limehouse."

"That old bastard?"

"He might be old, John, but he knows his stuff. He's had more of his boys go pro than any other trainer I know."

"Who is this boy?" asked John.

"Tyler."

"Is that his first name or his last name?" asked John.

"It's Tyler Thomson, John."

"Right. So make sure Old Man McGee doesn't get wind of this. He'll know people who know people, and if he finds out we're putting his boy up against Dixon's in a fight to the death, he'll bring the bleeding house down on us, and we'll all be putting wagers on cockroach races in Pentonville bleeding prison."

The phone on John's desk lit up, but the ringer was set to silent. John answered the call but said nothing.

"Boss, you might want to come down here," said Northern Mike, John's pub manager. "You've had a delivery."

John replaced the handset and stood up from his seat. He threw on his jacket then pulled his cuffs and cufflinks down so they showed. His tailor-made shirts and jackets were all cut to show an inch of white cuff, just enough for his diamond cufflinks to make a statement and to offer a glint of his platinum Breitling watch.

"Let's go, boys," he said. "Mike reckons we have a delivery."

The three men, led by John, made their way down the rear stairs of the Golden Ring and through a door that opened out into the family side of the pub. The muffled sounds of men laughing and talking with the percussive chink of pint glasses being washed and stacked came from the bar next door.

At the entrance, Jeff the Plumber, one of the regulars, held the door open, letting in the cold night air. Outside on the pavement, Northern Mike was hunched over a man lying on the ground. He looked up as John approached and shook his head, his face solemn.

The body of Blake Green lay on the wet ground. His lifeless eyes stared up at John.

"Get him inside, boys," said John to Mick and Jack, then he checked the street for nosy passers-by.

They hauled the huge man inside by his arms and dropped his lifeless body on the carpet beside the fruit machine.

"I just found him like it, John," said Jeff, as he shut the doors and slid the bolts to lock them. "I don't know how long he'd been there."

"Did you see anyone else? Any cars?"

"Nothing, John. I swear."

"Alright, mate," replied John. He flicked five twenty pound notes off a roll of cash bound with a silver money clip and stuffed them into Jeff's top pocket. "Do me a favour, yeah?"

"I won't say anything, John. You know me."

"I do, Jeff. Thanks, mate. We'll take it from here. Tell Debbie to put your drinks on my tab."

Jeff slipped past the group of men and through the door, letting the noise of the public bar fill the space for a few seconds. Then it faded as the door closed. Northern Mike locked it and turned to face John.

"Do you know him, John?" he asked.

John nodded.

"Yes, Mike, I do." He thought for a few seconds then verbalised his plan.

"Right, Jack, get this pile of crap out the back and into the motor. Dump him in Epping Forest. Somewhere he'll be found by a dog walker. Mick, as soon as you see the discovery on the news, pay his wife a visit. Slip her five grand in an envelope."

He turned to the pub manager.

"Mike?"

Northern Mike looked up from the body at their feet.

"Boss?" he replied.

"Get this bleeding carpet cleaned up. Not a trace. Understood?"

Northern Mike nodded, but he looked hesitant.

John placed a reassuring hand on Mike's shoulder, just as his phone vibrated in his pocket. The number was blocked and the small screen read '*Unknown Caller,*' but he didn't need to be a rocket scientist to know who it was.

He hit the green button to answer the call and waited for the familiar gravelly voice.

"Checkmate," said Dixon.

CHAPTER FIFTEEN

"How did it go?" asked Melody. "Did you find it?"

"Yeah, I did," replied Harvey.

"So are you coming back to Reg's place? We're going out for dinner tonight. The wedding is in two days and they want to say thanks."

"Yeah, I'll be back," said Harvey. He switched the lights off, pulled the car to the side of the road and watched as the man in the hat disappeared through a doorway beside some shops.

"Okay, but don't be too long," said Melody. "This means a lot to them."

"I'll be back soon," said Harvey. "I'm just finishing something."

He disconnected the call, turned the car off and waited. As if on cue, a few light raindrops dotted the windscreen. The street lights ahead magnified and fragmented the light but Harvey's eyes remained fixed on the doors. A light flicked on in a first-floor window and a figure passed across the frame but too fast for Harvey to see who it was. A few minutes later, the light flicked off.

Ahead of where Harvey had parked, on the opposite side of the road, a black BMW pulled over outside the doors Harvey was watching. The lights flicked off and the plume of smoke faded into the night. A van pulled into the street behind the car; for a brief moment, its headlights washed across it and silhouetted two men sitting in the front.

A flash of lightning lit the sky in Harvey's rear-view mirror. The light patter of rain on the car's bodywork grew into heavy drumming as the downpour began and the windscreen was obscured. Harvey turned on the ignition and cracked the car's electric window, but in the narrow field of view, all he saw was the door. It was closing. He flicked the windscreen wipers on to see the struggle of the two men forcing someone into the back of the BMW.

Harvey reached for the door handle, but it was too late. The BMW doors slammed, the engine fired up, and the headlights lit the street as the driver planted his foot to the floor and sped out of the parking spot. Harvey bent down out of sight, started the engine of Melody's little sports car, dipped the clutch, and found first gear. By the time the BMW had shot past, Harvey was accelerating out of his parking spot in the opposite direction. In his mirror, he saw the BMW turn left on the highway, so Harvey dropped into second, lifted the clutch and let the gearbox slow the car to make the turn. As soon as the car nosed out of the bend, Harvey slammed down the accelerator. It had been years since he'd been in the neighbourhood but he knew the streets well.

At the first crossroads, Harvey wrenched the wheel to the right. The highway was at the end of the street; he was only halfway down it when the BMW flashed past, faster than the other cars on the road. Harvey slid onto the highway, nosing between two cars and upsetting the driver behind. The BMW was four hundred yards in front. The highway was the main artery into the City of London and traffic was monitored. Harvey settled in and focused on the rear lights of the BMW in front.

His phone vibrated in his pocket and Melody's number flashed up. He put the phone away, checked his mirrors and closed the distance between him and the BMW.

The lights of the Limehouse Link tunnel loomed ahead, bright like a portal in the night. The BMW entered it, followed thirty seconds later by Harvey in Melody's little Mazda. A van and a taxi travelled side by side at the same pace to avoid the speed cameras in the tunnel. But the BMW was moving fast, not slowing for the cameras. Harvey eased the Mazda behind the taxi in a signal that he wanted to pass. But the taxi driver entered a power game and held fast. Aware of the bright lights illuminating Melody's very identifiable car, Harvey hung back behind the van but watched the BMW through the long, sweeping bends until, at last, the end of the tunnel was in sight. The car broke free into the rain and the darkness.

By the time the taxi, the van and Harvey left the tunnel, the BMW was nowhere to be seen.

Rain pelted the car once more. Canary Wharf and the Isle of Dogs were on Harvey's right. Another road merged at the tunnel exit. All Harvey could see were dozens of tail lights of the cars ahead, magnified and distorted by the rain, and unidentifiable in the dark. The taxi eventually moved into the next lane and Harvey accelerated past him.

Half a mile in front, Harvey knew there was a junction, where the BMW would be lost for sure. Before that was a slip road off to the left; a few cars in the left-hand lane were taking it. Harvey studied the tail lights but recognised none as the BMW. He kept looking at the cars as he drove onto the slip road and rose up onto an overpass, but saw nothing.

He slowed for the junction, scouring the cars that peeled off and the others that waited for a gap. But again, he saw nothing. He joined a group of cars three lanes wide and three cars back from the roundabout. He pulled to a stop. While everyone else was looking right for a gap, Harvey looked left, and came face to face with the driver of the BMW. He feigned disinterest, saw a space in the traffic, waited for the BMW to join the flow, and then slipped in behind it.

The BMW had slowed down, a move that Harvey presumed was to avoid being stopped by the police with a kidnapped man in the back. It turned onto East India Dock Road, matched the speed of the traffic and remained inconspicuous until it turned off Prince Regent Lane, where the driver found the maze of back streets and opened up the engine.

To follow them directly in Melody's little convertible would have been too obvious. Knowing the streets well, Harvey took the next left and caught up to them as the driver parked outside the Golden Ring Pub. Plaistow had been Harvey's stomping ground when he and Julios had worked for Harvey's foster father, John Cartwright. The only time Harvey had ever been in the Golden Ring was to find a man who owed John money.

They'd waited in the car park. It was rare that Harvey and Julios would talk while they stalked their prey. There was never much to be said, and Julios' ethos was to remain focused at all times. It was a testament to the length of his career. Until the end. And then it was Harvey who had been distracted.

Harvey drove past the pub, turned into a side street, killed the lights, and switched off the engine. He got out of the car, leaving the doors unlocked to avoid the flash of the indicators, and edged to the end of the road, out of sight. The muffle of men's voices followed. Then the dull thud of body blows and accompanying groans were the only sounds Harvey heard above the rain splashing in the puddles and hitting the roofs of parked cars. He watched from afar as one of the two men held the door of the pub open. The other marched the kidnapped guy inside at gunpoint.

To pull a gun in the open street, regardless of the time of night and torrential rain, was a brave move. Either things had changed since Harvey had worked the area or these men ran the neighbourhood. Harvey presumed the latter, which would mean there would be more men.

The phone in his pocket vibrated. It was Melody. It had to be.

She was the only person who ever called him. He ignored the call, pulled his jacket around him, and marched across the street. He looked both ways, but the road was quiet and nobody had seen him.

He stepped into the Golden Ring.

CHAPTER SIXTEEN

"Sit down," said the man with the silver hair. He was dressed well in an expensive-looking shirt, smart trousers and shiny shoes. A nice watch peeked from his cuff and he sat relaxed in an armchair beside the fire as if he owned the place.

Tyler checked around the room. Although the bar next door sent a hum of activity through the adjoining door, the room Tyler had been brought into was empty, save for the two men who had picked him up, and the old man in the chair.

"I'd rather stand," said Tyler. "This won't take long, will it?"

"It'll take as long as I want it to take, and it'll be quicker if you do as you're told," said the man. "So sit down." He held out a hand, offering the chair opposite him. "Mick, get the boy a drink, will you? What do you want, son?"

"I don't drink," said Tyler, unable to meet the man's eyes.

"Another one that doesn't bleeding drink. What is with you people?"

Sensing the question was rhetorical, Tyler remained silent. He studied the intricate patterns of the old carpet at his feet.

"Let me introduce myself," said the old man. "You can call me John." He held out his hand once more, this time for Tyler to shake. Short, fat, ringed fingers gripped Tyler's hand with a positive strength. The shake was barely perceptible; John allowed the squeeze to do the talking.

"Look, John," said Tyler, "I haven't done nothing wrong. I don't know who you are, but honestly, I haven't done anything."

"I know, son. I know." John raised his hand. "Don't worry. You're not in any kind of trouble."

"So what am I doing here?" asked Tyler. "This bloke shoved a gun in my face." He jerked his thumb at Mick who placed a bottle of sparkling water on the table in front of him.

"No harm done, Tyler," said John. "I'm sure it was all meant in good spirit." He eyed the man he'd called Mick and nodded. It was a slight movement, enough to reassure his subordinate that he'd done the right thing.

"How's your mum, Tyler? I hear she's ill."

"What? How do you know about-"

"Look," said John, his face twisted as if he'd had enough of the back and forth, "let's clear up any ambiguity, shall we? Then perhaps we can move onto business."

"Business?" asked Tyler.

"I'm a very well-known man, and a very well-known man knows lots of people. It's my business to be in the know. So anything I know about you shouldn't come as a surprise. Now, I know that your old mum is sick, and I asked how she was."

"Today was a good day," Tyler replied.

"A good day? Well that's something," said John. "Tell me what a bad day looks like."

Tyler felt his throat close and his eyes bulge as the memories showed themselves to him alone.

"Delirious. Incontinent. Passing blood, vomiting blood, and pained to the point of pulling her own hair out of her head and clawing at her skin to get to the pain." He paused. "Shall I go on?"

John held his gaze, his expression serious. Regardless of the surroundings, he seemed somehow empathetic.

"That's a lot for a boy your age to deal with."

"I'm not a boy and I'm dealing with it the best I can."

"That's admirable," said John, with an accompanying smile. "I hear you're a boxer?"

Tyler nodded. "Yeah. I'm supposed to be there now. My trainer won't be happy. He's giving me extra time in the ring."

"Personal attention from Old Man McGee?" said John. "You are privileged."

"You know him?"

John laughed. "Yeah. Anyone who's anyone in this world knows the old man. Does he still have that big guy mopping up after him?"

"Lloyd? Yeah, he's still there. Look, is this going to take long? I don't want-"

"I know. You don't want the old man to think you've skipped a training session and wasted his time. That's okay. We can take care of the old man for you. I'll tell him you're with me."

"No," said Tyler, a little brash. "It should come from me. Are we done?"

"No, Tyler, we are not done. I'll get Mick here to drop you at the arches when we're finished. How does that sound?"

It was only then that Tyler turned to look at Mick and recognised him as the man from the gym the previous night. He turned again and eyed the man by the door. It was both of them.

"What do you want with me, John?"

"Simple," said John. He leaned forwards, resting his elbows on his knees, then collected his brandy from the small table between them. "I want to put you in the ring, son."

"I can't do it," replied Tyler. "The old man-"

"Yeah, yeah. The old man said you can't fight for anyone else or he'll stop training you. So what? From what I hear, you don't need him anymore anyway. Look at the bleeding size of you."

"I can't let him down."

John listened and nodded.

"So much honour. But so little brains," he said. Then he sat back with his glass of brandy and took a sip without removing his eyes from Tyler's. "What if I told you that the winnings would get your mum private medical attention? No more of this waiting around for some old fart on the National Health Service to procrastinate and worry about making a decision. You could afford to let the professionals look after her."

"I can't do it," said Tyler. "The old man-"

"Sod the old man, Tyler. Think about your poor old mum. Delirious, you said. In so much pain she's clawing at her own skin. You could stop that, Tyler. Look at me when I'm talking to you, son."

Tyler looked up from the floor. He felt his eyes redden.

"Don't be ashamed, Tyler. Be proud of who you are." John took a sip of his brandy. "She's dying, isn't she?"

A single tear rolled down Tyler's cheek. He bit his bottom lip.

"Let it go, Tyler," said John. "I'm giving you the chance to stop it, son. No-one knows how long she has left, do they?"

Tyler shook his head. At the same time, the door opened and a man entered. Tyler glanced up to see who it was, but tears fogged his vision. He let his head drop back down. His silent tears fell to the floor. John leaned forwards and spoke quietly.

"So here's your chance to make her last days as nice as possible."

CHAPTER SEVENTEEN

"Sorry, mate, this bar is shut. You'll have to go next door," said Jack, who was leaning on the bar with a pint.

The man let the door swing closed behind him, looked around the room, and let his gaze fall on Tyler, who was wiping his eyes.

"It's a bit noisy for me next door," replied the man. He took three strides towards the bar where he stood with his back to John and Tyler, and with Mick and Jack to his right.

"I said the bar is closed, sunshine," said Jack. "You'll need to go next door to get a drink."

"And I said it's a bit too noisy for me next door," replied the man.

John grinned at Jack's failed attempt to impress him. He glanced back at John, embarrassed by the lack of fear he'd instilled into the man.

"Listen, pal, you've got five seconds to get out or-"

"Or what?" said the man. He turned to face Jack, but his stance wasn't threatening. In fact, it was as casual as if he was waiting at a bar for a beer.

John sipped at his brandy and admired the man's control.

"That's five seconds. The way I see it, it's you who has options.

You can either try to throw me out in the pouring rain." He held his arms up as if he was waiting for Jack to make a move, then dropped them to his sides and rolled his neck from side to side. "Or you can shut up and leave me to dry off."

The two men stared each other down. The anger was clear in Jack's eyes, but still, the stranger remained unmoved. Northern Mike appeared through the service door that linked to the two bars. He glanced at the stranger and at John.

"Another brandy, John?" he called out, ignoring the standoff between Jack and the man.

"Why not?" John replied. "And can you get our friend here a drink and a towel or something please, Mike?"

A towel landed on the bar beside the stranger, then Mike's face appeared beside him.

"What can I get you, mate?" he asked.

"Water's fine," came the reply.

A bottle of sparkling water was placed beside the towel. Mike brought the brandy to John's table.

"Mick, do me a favour. Take Jack for a walk in the rain. He looks like he could do with cooling off."

"I don't need a-" began Jack.

"Jack, go for a walk," said John. "Mick, go with him."

A look of contempt flashed across Mick's face. He pulled his coat on and threw Jack's to him, a little harder than necessary.

When the door swung closed and the sound of the rain was quietened, the stranger turned and leaned on the bar. He nodded once at Northern Mike, then cracked the lid off the water bottle. In the mirror behind the optics, John found the stranger staring at him.

"Can I go now?" asked Tyler.

John broke the stare and addressed Tyler.

"So you're going to do it?"

"Can you make it so that the old man doesn't find out about it?" replied Tyler. "He's been good to me, and, well-"

"Listen, son. You leave the old man to me. Meet me here

tomorrow night. Six o'clock. Bring your gear. We'll get you in the ring and see what you're made of."

"And can I ask what I get?" said Tyler. "I mean, if I win. What's the pay-out?"

"What if I said fifty grand?" replied John, taking another sip of his third or fourth brandy.

The eyebrows on Tyler's face rose, showing bright red lines in the backs of his eyes.

"Is that enough?" asked John.

"I'm in," replied Tyler. He leaned across the table to shake John's hand. A smile of hope spread across his face. He sat back in his seat, cracked the water bottle with shaky hands and took a long mouthful. But then a thought hit him. His expression changed to curiosity. "Do I need to sign anything? Are there insurance papers I need to sign? I had to do that before, for my last fight."

"Your word is good enough for me," replied John. He sank his brandy and felt the satisfying burn as it made its way down his gullet. "People rarely let me down, Tyler."

"I need to think about it. What happens if I say no?" Tyler asked.

John set his glass on the table. He leaned in, beckoning Tyler to meet him halfway, and lowered his voice to a whisper.

"We just made a deal, Tyler. If you back out now, they'll be scraping bits of your poor old mum off the kitchen wall for a week. Do I make myself clear?"

CHAPTER EIGHTEEN

The phone in Harvey's pocket vibrated. He couldn't ignore it any longer. With a nod of thanks to the man sitting by the fireplace, Harvey pulled the phone out and stepped outside into the rain. He checked both directions and crossed the street.

"Harvey, where are you?" asked Melody. "You said you'd be back."

"I'm coming back now," he replied. "I stopped to see someone."

"See who? You've been gone hours, Harvey."

"Well, I'm coming back now. Get yourself ready to go out. I'll be thirty minutes."

Harvey disconnected the call and turned into the side street where he'd parked Melody's car. Something wasn't right. The way the car was sitting was off; it was leaning to one side. He edged along the wall of the end-of-terrace house and saw the huge frame of the boy sitting in the passenger seat.

Harvey stepped into view and, although the street was dark and any moonlight was blocked by the heavy clouds, he saw the white face of the boy turn towards him through the rain-spattered glass.

The door opened and the car's suspension seemed to sigh with relief as he eased one long leg out of the small vehicle and pulled himself out into the rain. The boy towered over Harvey and was nearly twice as wide, but his hands fumbled with a nervous energy as if they sought something to do.

"I'm sorry," said the boy. "I saw you park here. That's how I knew it was your car."

"So you sat in it?" said Harvey.

"The way you spoke to them in there. You wasn't scared. They're dangerous. One of them had a gun."

Harvey studied the boy's proportions.

"Having a gun is one thing. Using it is another. And using it properly is another thing altogether."

The boy was silent.

"It's Tyler, isn't it?" asked Harvey. "I heard that bloke call you Tyler."

The boy nodded.

"You want my advice?" said Harvey.

Another silent and ashamed nod.

"Run away. Get away from them and don't look back," said Harvey. "You seem like a good kid. But if you carry on with those guys, it's the beginning of the end. Trust me."

Tyler's face seemed to drop as if every muscle in it had relented to the pressure of holding back the emotion.

"I'm in trouble," he said. His voice had raised an octave. "I don't know what I've got myself into."

Harvey watched the boy fight his emotions, but didn't try to stop him. Instead, he checked both ways in the dark street then sighed.

"Get in the car," said Harvey.

He walked around to the driver's side, opened the door and climbed in. The sheer width of Tyler's frame occupied most of the space inside and when Harvey pulled his door closed, the two men's shoulders had nowhere to go but rest against each other.

"How do you know them?" asked Harvey. He started the engine and set the fan to clear the windscreen, which was fogging up.

"I don't know them. They came out of nowhere. I left my flat to go to training and they jumped me. They hit me and put a gun in my face."

"And you didn't fight back?"

"I wanted to," said Tyler. He stared out of the windscreen, his eyes shining in the dark. "I should have, but..."

"But what?" asked Harvey. "If two guys jump me, I fight back. I'm guessing you're strong. You could have handled them."

"Not with the gun. Plus, I'm not allowed."

"You're not allowed to fight back when two men put a gun in your face?"

"I did it once before. I hurt someone pretty bad," said Tyler. "The police arrested me, but the guy came around in the end and they dropped the charges."

"Came around?" asked Harvey.

"He was in a coma."

"You put him in a coma?"

"I didn't mean to. I only hit him once or twice, not a lot."

"You can't remember?" asked Harvey. "Is it hazy?"

Tyler nodded. "I remember it, but the details are cloudy, like..." Tyler searched for the right words. "It's like I was drunk, but I wasn't. I don't drink."

"It's okay. I know what you mean. But you need to control that. You need to channel the anger and control it."

"That's what I did earlier. I held it back."

"You held it back and had a gun put in your face, then you were chucked into a car and driven off. That's not channelling the anger. That's called being kidnapped, Tyler. You need to take that energy, but instead of suppressing it, you need to drive it to where you want it to be. When you feel that anger coming on and all you want to do is hurt someone, you need to remember your training. You need to go back to basics and let that anger bubble away in the background. Don't push it away but don't let it overtake your training."

The two sat in silence for a moment. A car drove past and its headlights flashed across the dashboard.

"You sound like you have it too," said Tyler. "The temper."

"It's not a temper," replied Harvey. He questioned if he should continue; he'd already said too much. But the boy was genuine, and he had a familiarity that had caught Harvey's attention. "I don't know what it is, but you're right, it's inside me."

"How did you learn to control it?"

The question came out of nowhere. It shouldn't have. Harvey should have seen it coming. But it hit him hard.

He didn't reply.

"Did you end up in trouble like me? Is that it?" asked Tyler.

"Somebody showed me, Tyler. Somebody saw it in me and helped me."

Harvey's phone began to vibrate once more. He put his hand in his pocket.

"Can you help me?" asked Tyler. "I mean, do you think you could? I can fight, but I'm in trouble. If I lose my temper, it'll all be over."

"I'm not the man you need, Tyler. Trust me."

"I do," said Tyler. "I don't know why. I don't know you. But do you think you can show me how to channel it? Or at least get me started? I could pay. I have money, a little."

"I'm not the man you need, Tyler," said Harvey. "Nobody needs advice from me."

He put the car in gear and pulled his phone from his pocket.

"You can get out here, or I can drop you on the way. That's about all I can do for you," said Harvey. He hit the green button on his phone.

"One second, Melody." He looked across at Tyler. "What do you want to do?"

"It was you, wasn't it?" said Tyler. "Earlier?"

Harvey didn't reply.

"I saw you. I know it was you."

"Where?"

Tyler looked at his feet again and scratched at his hand.

"At my dad's grave."

CHAPTER NINETEEN

"So I was wondering if maybe we could talk, you know, about my Dad," said Tyler, as Harvey pulled the little Mazda up to the entrance of Tyler's building.

"There's not a lot I can tell you," replied Harvey.

"It doesn't have to be a lot. It doesn't have to be much at all. It's weird, but I feel this connection to him somehow through you."

Harvey didn't reply.

"Can I call you? Or you could call me? I don't know anything really. I only know what he looked like from photos and Mum doesn't say much about him. She shuts down if I mention his name."

There was a naivety in the boy's language that Julios wouldn't have tolerated, but also a softness in his eyes. There was no denying the boy was Julios' son. Harvey could see it in his size, and his features in profile with the large square jaw, piercing eyes and an over-sized nose.

"You can call me," said Harvey. "Do you have a pen?"

Tyler rummaged through his bag and wrote Harvey's number on the back of his hand.

"It really means a lot to me. Thank you for this."

"I'm in London for a few days. After that, I'll be gone and I doubt I'll be back."

"I'll call. I promise," said Tyler. "Can I ask one thing?"

Harvey's eyebrows raised in anticipation.

"Can I ask what your name is? You didn't say and maybe my mum knows of you."

"Your mum doesn't know me," replied Harvey. "What's her name?"

"Leah. Her name's Leah Thomson."

Harvey didn't reply.

"She knew all the faces around here. Anyone that was worth knowing, that is. She was married to some gangster bloke, but they were divorced before I was born. Mum said they got married too young. Mum started seeing my dad, on the quiet, you know? She wouldn't have people talking about her."

"And what happened to the gangster?" asked Harvey.

"He was killed eventually. I guess when you walk that line you have to expect it might happen one day, right? Good riddance, I say."

"And you never met your dad?"

"No, he stopped coming round but used to send mum money. It's weird. It was as if she didn't want him there, but she never speaks bad of him, not like the other fella, the gangster." Tyler paused. "Didn't he ever talk about me?"

"Your dad didn't say much at all, Tyler. He was a private man."

"I wish I knew him. From what Mum says, he was a great man. But he just couldn't commit to us. It's weird though, a couple of times while I was on my way to school or out with my mates, I'd imagine I saw him driving past or walking nearby. But whenever I looked again, he'd be gone. It's almost as if some part of me wanted him to be there."

"How long have you been going to the grave?"

"A few years now. Mum found out where it was and told me. I don't really know why I go. I guess it's just a connection. I talk to him about mum and about my training." A solitary, weak laugh broke Tyler's memories. "He's a good listener."

Harvey left Tyler with his thoughts for a few seconds and considered what to say. For the first time in a long while, there was so much Harvey wanted to say, but there was also so much he couldn't. A memory here and there might open the boy's wounds. But nothing might close him off, and he was the closest Harvey had to having his old friend back.

"I should go," said Tyler. He reached for the door handle and glanced through the windscreen at the torrential rain. He turned back to Harvey as he pulled on the door handle. "Thanks. I *will* call you, maybe tomorrow."

"Wait," said Harvey. He'd started. He couldn't stop now. "Close the door."

Tyler pulled the door shut and the interior light flicked off.

"Do you want to know about your dad?" asked Harvey. "I didn't know my dad either. I know what it's like, the wondering."

"Anything," replied Tyler, his eyes wide in the semi-light of the dark street.

"My dad was killed. My mum too. We were fostered by a man, not far from here. I don't remember it happening. I was just a baby. But my sister and I were taken in by this man and his wife. It was the same man your dad worked for. He was his security."

"Like a minder or a bodyguard?" asked Tyler.

"Exactly that," replied Harvey. "I ended up in some trouble. I was heading the wrong way, probably just like a million other boys out there right now. But my foster father asked Julios to take me under his wing, you know, show me a better path."

Tyler nodded. His eyes glistened at Harvey mentioning his dad as if the words had added a reality to the name, the photos and the grave marker.

"I was only young, about thirteen years old, I think. Maybe older. He started to train me, taught me to swim, made me run and do push-ups. All the things a kid hates, right?"

"Right," said Tyler with another single laugh enthused with an anxious energy.

"Then he started to teach me defence. I loved it. I ended up spending more time with your old man than my own foster father. We grew very close."

"So he taught you to fight?" asked Tyler.

"He taught me a lot of things, Tyler. Yeah, fighting was one aspect of it. But it was more than that. The fighting, the training and exercise, it all came second to a mindset, a way of thinking."

"What do you mean?"

Harvey turned in his seat and edged into the corner, allowing him to see Tyler without turning his head.

"Everything your dad ever did was part of a plan. If he put his keys on a table, he'd do it a certain way. If he opened a door, he did it a certain way."

"Why?" asked Tyler. "I mean, why open a door a certain way? How many ways are there?"

Harvey looked up at the street outside.

"Do you see that door there?" he asked.

"The green one?"

"How would you open it?"

"I'd pull the handle and walk inside."

"Who's on the other side?"

Tyler shrugged. "I don't know."

"Exactly."

"Was his job dangerous?" asked Tyler.

"Sometimes," replied Harvey, but redirecting the trail of conversation. "Everything he did was meticulous. Parking a car, he'd drive up and down the street twice before even attempting to park. Your dad was a smart man, and that mindset was habitual. It drove his life and he passed that on to me. I think, more than anything, that's what I learned most from him. The mindset."

"But you didn't drive up and down before you parked," said Tyler.

"I'd like to think that part of my life is over. What I'm trying to say, Tyler, and believe me, this is the hardest thing I've ever had to say, but your dad meant the world to me. More than anyone I ever met. If you turn out to be half the man he was, you're onto a winner."

Tears had overflowed the wells in Tyler's eyes and a single drop rolled down each of his cheeks.

"I'll call you tomorrow, yeah?" said Tyler. He gave Harvey a thoughtful look and hid his face, embarrassed by his tears.

Harvey didn't reply.

Just as the car door was about to slam, Tyler ducked inside once more. Harvey had straightened and put the car into first gear.

"You didn't tell me your name," said Tyler.

Harvey stared back at him, considering the consequences and weighing up the odds. But his affection broke through the defences that the boy's father had taught him.

"Harvey," he said. "Harvey Stone."

CHAPTER TWENTY

It took just a few seconds for the downpour to soak Tyler through. He looked up at the windows of his flat. The lights were off. If his mum had been up, he'd see the flickering of the TV through the kitchen window. It was a trick he'd learned as a kid when he'd stayed out too late.

He pulled his hood up as Harvey drove away and checked to see if he looked in his mirror, but the rain, the dark and the tiny window made it impossible to see.

Tyler watched the little Mazda drive to the end of the street, where it turned right onto the highway towards Tower Bridge. Tyler turned and fumbled in his pocket for his keys, but as he did, a shadow stepped out of the neighbouring doorway, broad and as black as the night.

The movement caught Tyler off guard, and he stumbled backwards. The man moved towards him, his hands in his jacket pockets and a dark hood pulled over his head, which covered half of his face.

"You let him down, Tyler."

It was only when the man spoke that Tyler's fear sank further into a sense of dread, a tightening at the bottom of his stomach.

"Lloyd, I can explain."

"So explain," replied Lloyd. "Do you know how many people get the chance you had? You missed training, Tyler. Would you rather be out with your mates than-"

"It's not what you think, Lloyd. Honest. I can explain."

"So tell me," said Lloyd.

Tyler took another glance up to the windows.

"Shall we talk inside?" asked Tyler.

Lloyd looked up too, and then shook his head.

"I don't need to intrude. I just came to warn you. You have everything going for you, son. You have the talent and you have the trainer that will take you to the top. What you don't have is the mindset."

"Mindset?" said Tyler.

"Did I say something?" asked Lloyd.

Tyler was looking past him to where Harvey had disappeared around the corner.

"No," said Tyler. "No, I understand."

"Do you? Do you understand that right now, the old man is talking about not even letting you back in his gym, let alone training you."

"I told you," said Tyler. "Something came up. Family stuff."

"You can't kid a kidder," said Lloyd. "If there's one thing a lifetime of being around juveniles has taught me, it's how to spot a lie."

"It was," said Tyler. "Honest."

"And the man in the car was family, was he?"

Tyler fought to keep eye contact with Lloyd.

"Yeah. Yeah, he was, in a way."

"Training tomorrow. I'll talk to the old man, but it's the last time. You let us down again and you lose it all. And don't think any other gym will train you once the old man drops you. If you mess this up, that's it. That's your career in the ring over."

"Thanks, Lloyd. I won't let you down. I promise."

"Don't come by tomorrow. Let me talk to him. Come on Saturday night. Double session. Be prepared to work hard."

"I will," said Tyler. "No, wait. Saturday. I can't."

Lloyd cocked his head and even in the darkness beneath his hood, Tyler could see his eyes narrow.

"And why can't you come in on Saturday? You either want my help or you don't."

"I, erm, I said I'd help a friend."

"A friend?"

"Yeah. He's only in town for a few days and I said I'd-"

"Saturday night, Tyler. The old man won't wait any longer. What's more important to you?"

"Training, of course it is."

"So be there. I'm sure your friend has other friends to call on."

Lloyd finished with a cold, hard stare, which Tyler knew was him searching for sincerity.

"I'll be there," said Tyler. "Double session."

Lloyd turned away and pulled the collar of his jacket close to his neck as he walked.

"Hey, Lloyd," called Tyler. He'd been standing in the rain for more than ten minutes but had only just begun to feel the cold as the damp seeped through to his skin.

Lloyd turned but only a shadow beneath his hood looked back.

"Thanks, yeah?" said Tyler. "Thanks for your help."

Lloyd nodded once and slipped around the corner.

The entrance to the flats was still broken, but the front door was locked. Tyler let himself in, avoiding the noisy parts of the floor, just as he had for the past ten years since he'd been coming home late.

He switched the kettle on and grabbed his favourite mug from the cupboard. It was white with the words 'Education is important but boxing is importanter' in bold black letters. His mum had seen it in a cheap store and bought it for him back when she was able to go to the shops alone. He spooned in two spoonfuls of cocoa. It was a luxury he allowed himself after training, and although he hadn't trained that night, he felt he needed something to help him sleep.

A whining in his ear, relentless and monotone, sang through his head and he felt the familiar restless toe-tapping that came when he was anxious. While the kettle boiled, he removed his wet clothes, stripping to his shorts in the kitchen, and hung them over the radiator beneath the window. It was as he did so that he saw them. Two men sitting in a car outside the flat. The glow of a cigarette occasionally lit the dashboard in a weak orange light.

Tyler flicked the light switch and stepped back to the window.

"Maybe Harvey could help," he whispered to himself.

He dug his mobile phone from his bag and hit the on button. The little screen glowed in a green light. He held it beneath the window so he could watch the two men. He used the light to see his hand, where he'd written Harvey's number. But instead of the neat little numbers, he found a blue ink smudge across his skin. Only two of the digits even resembled numbers.

Tyler sank to his haunches with his back against the fridge and let his head fall down. There was no way he could find him now.

A car door closed outside. Tyler peeked through the window, but all he saw was the empty car with no orange glow of a cigarette lighting the dashboard.

CHAPTER TWENTY-ONE

"Did he say he'd do it, John?" asked Mick, as he poured himself and John a drink from behind the bar.

John was still sitting in his chair with the fire burning low, a bed of hot embers pulsing with rage beside him. He waited for Mick to hand him a drink, took a sip, puckered his lips then set the glass down on the table.

"Of course he did," replied John. "You leave the boy to me. What I want you and Jack to do is give the opposition a disadvantage."

"You mean you want us to take his boy out?" asked Mick. "What was his name?"

"Mackie," said John. The name was at the forefront of his thoughts.

"That's it," said Mick. "Do you want us to take care of him?"

"No, no. Dixon already played that card. He'll be expecting a retaliation. No, that's not the way. You see, while you two were out for a stroll in the rain, I did a bit of thinking. Brandy's good for that, Mick, thinking. There's nothing quite like being warmed by an open fire and sipping at a nice brandy to keep the creative juices flowing."

"You've had some ideas then?" said Mick. He rubbed his hands together and turned one of the chairs opposite John to face the fire, then laid his jacket across the back to dry it out.

"Tyler Thomson," said John. "That's our boy. I haven't seen anyone that big for a long time, and if he can fight like I've been told he can fight, then we're rock solid, Mick. Rock solid."

"I hear good things, John. The old man wouldn't be wasting his time training a nobody."

"No, Mick. No, he wouldn't. But, you see, the old man can't give the boy the training he needs. What that boy needs, the thing that will take him to the top, is up here in the grey matter, Mick." John tapped at his temple with his index finger. "He doesn't have the killer instinct. Not yet anyway. But if he gets through this fight, he'll be a changed man."

"If he gets through this fight, he'll be a killer, John. A thing like that can really affect somebody, mentally, I mean."

"You mean *when* he comes through this fight, and he will. Nothing hardens someone up better than a few sleepless nights of restless remorse. If he comes out the other side unscathed, he'll be unstoppable, and he'll be someone we'll want on our side. He'll be going places and he'll have yours truly to thank for his success."

"So you haven't told him it's a fight to the death?" asked Mick. "He thinks it's just a normal boxing match?"

"Of course I haven't," said John. "He doesn't even know it's bare-knuckle, but he won't back out now. Besides, the bloke was in bits already. I don't know which one of you hit him or how hard you did it, but you scared the hell out of the kid."

"It was Jack. He always gets carried away," said Mick.

"Well, young Jack wants to control it. He's not as tough as he thinks he is. Did you see that muppet walk in here earlier? All the poor bloke wanted was to get out of the rain and Jack starts mouthing off and giving him stick trying to impress me. Giving someone a hard time isn't going to impress me, especially when that someone happens to shut him down. Now, if Jack decided to stick one on him, that would impress me. Anyway, pissing people off is one sure-fire way to bring attention to the place. He's got to learn how to treat people. Mark my words, Mick, *when* young Tyler gets through this *and* handles the ensuing nightmares, he's going to be a monster, and that monster will remember the beating that Jack gave him way back when. I'd like to be there for that one."

"Do you want me to have a word with him?" asked Mick. "You know, calm him down a bit?"

John reached for his drink, shifted in his seat, and shook his head.

"No, Mick. In matters such as these, I prefer to let nature take its course."

"So how are we going to get at Dixon's boy?"

"Ah, we digressed," said John. He felt a smile warm the muscles on his face. "Like I said, Mick, it's all in the mind. Find out who he is. Where he's from. He must have family. He must have a weak point. Find it and bring it to me. We've got two days until the fight so I want something to work with by tomorrow night at the latest. We're going to break that boy from the inside out and there won't be a thing Dixon can do to stop us until it's too late."

"What about the old man?" asked Mick.

John's left eye twitched at the question. It was an annoyance, a potential thorn in his side.

"Take care of it, Mick."

CHAPTER TWENTY-TWO

"Oh my god, Harvey, where have you been?" said Melody.

She looked up at him, concerned and with a glass of wine in her hand, then quietened when she saw the look on his face.

The waiter pulled his chair for him, but Harvey issued him a look that told the man he didn't require assistance to sit down. He seated himself and collected a menu from the centre of the table. Melody took it from him with her spare hand.

"What happened?" she whispered.

Harvey didn't reply.

"Can I get you a drink, sir?" asked the waiter.

"Water's fine," replied Harvey, and he glanced around the room, where tables of twos and fours hosted couples and foursomes. The new couples laughed and were lost in their own little worlds. The seasoned couples sat in near silence. The foursomes each battled with two streams of conversation, fighting to be heard above the other.

There were no lone diners and no groups of men that rang alarm bells, but still, Harvey positioned his chair with its back to the wall to maintain a full view of the room. It was an old habit he'd never be able to break.

"We didn't think you'd come," said Jess. "But Melody said you wouldn't miss it."

The waiter delivered his water to the table, then cracked the lid and offered Harvey a slice of lemon. He refused the lemon and poured his own water.

"Don't you ever drink?" Jess asked.

"I never have done. I got this far without it. It would be a shame to start now."

"Harvey has never had alcohol and never worn anything apart from a white t-shirt," said Reg, offering Harvey a smile to let him know he was only joking.

Melody sidled up beside Harvey and worked herself under his arm.

"But he sure knows how to wear those white t-shirts, Reg," she said, and winked at Jess, running a playful hand down Harvey's chest.

"Well, I hope you brought a suit or something for the wedding," said Reg.

Harvey looked at Melody for a response.

"He's got a suit. He scrubs up well," said Melody.

"So, Harvey, how did it go? Did you find your friend?"

"My friend?" said Harvey, a little too brash.

"She means Julios," said Melody.

"Yeah, I found Julios. It was a little anticlimactic, but at least I know where he is. Thanks for arranging that. I hope you didn't have to break any rules," he said with a smile.

"It was nothing," replied Jess.

"So are you guys all set for the big day?" asked Harvey. "I feel I missed all the conversation."

"That's okay," said Reg. "We know how much he meant to you, Harvey."

Harvey offered Reg a curt nod.

"And yeah, we're all set," Reg continued. "In two days' time, we'll be Mr and Mrs Tenant."

"What about the honeymoon?" asked Harvey. "Have you made big plans?"

Reg and Jess looked at each other and the table fell silent.

"Well, we kind of spent everything we had on the flat, the wedding and the van."

"I've offered them our house for a few weeks," said Melody. "We'll stay here and they can enjoy the beach and the fields."

It wasn't often Melody drew a line in the sand with Harvey, but he knew her tone when she had.

"Okay," he said, realising that their little pocket of paradise in southern France would be more memorable than a wet weekend in Clapham. "You'll love it. The mornings are crisp and the sea's cold, but I've never experienced peace like it."

"We can't wait. It feels like I haven't had a holiday for years sometimes," said Jess. "It can't be healthy, going to work in the dark and coming home in the dark, only to wake up a few hours later to do it all over. A few weeks by the sea is exactly what we need."

"Excuse me," said Harvey. "I'll just find the washroom."

The conversation faded as he made his way between the tables, past the reception and into the toilets, where he splashed cool water onto his face. He leaned on the basin and stared at his reflection, pondering the small talk. He loved Reg and Jess but somehow never managed to fit into any of their conversations. He thought of the two men on the table of four, probably discussing business or sport, while their wives chatted about plans for children. He let out a long exhale then dried his hands and face using a rolled-up towel from a neat pile on the marble surface.

From the washroom door, he looked out across the restaurant. In the far corner, Jess, Reg and Melody were all discussing wedding plans, a subject on which he could offer no real input. To Harvey's right was the reception, a small counter with a cash register up top and small TV below showing a London news program. A reporter was standing beneath an umbrella in the rain as firefighters behind her rallied to put out a huge fire. The scene was lit by the flashing blue lights of emergency vehicles while the fire cast an orange haze over the surrounding cars and buildings.

The receptionist saw Harvey staring at the TV, and with an apologetic smile, she moved to switch it off.

"Wait," said Harvey. "Where is this?"

"Poplar," said the girl. "It's been burning for a while. I think it's the arches."

"Can you turn the volume up?" asked Harvey as ambulances arrived on the scene.

"Sorry, sir, I'm not really allowed to have it on."

He glanced back at the table where Melody, Reg and Jess were still absorbed in conversation.

"Can you do me a favour?" he asked, pulling his phone from his pocket. "Do you have a pen and paper?"

On the paper the receptionist slid across the counter, Harvey wrote the words 'I'm sorry.' He placed his phone in the centre of the paper and folded it into a parcel, then slid it towards the girl.

"Can you wait five minutes, and then deliver this to the table in the corner?"

CHAPTER TWENTY-THREE

"Mum, you need to get up," said Tyler, nudging his sleeping mother's shoulder. "Come on. Wake up, Mum."

Tyler flicked the lights on as she stirred and pulled the covers over her face.

"Come on, Mum. Wake up," he said with a little more urgency.

"What time is it?" she mumbled, just as there was a gentle knock on the front door.

"Mum, I'll explain later. But you need to wake up." He pulled the covers from her face then began to pull clothes from the cupboard and stuff them into a bag. Shielding her eyes from the light, his mum sat up and swung her legs out of the bed.

"What's going on?" she asked.

"Put your slippers on, Mum. There's no time to explain."

Another knock, louder than the first.

"Who's that at the door?" his mum asked.

"Mum, please," said Tyler. He could feel the frustration sending his heart rate skyward.

"Okay, okay. No need to rush me," she said, as she pushed herself to a standing position. Tyler helped to steady her, a little harder than usual.

"Easy, Tyler. I'm not as young as I used to be," she said. "Now, where are my slippers?"

Three hard knocks on the front door.

"Who is that at this time of night?"

Tyler finished stuffing his mother's medication into the bag, then dropped it on the bed and took hold of her shoulders.

"Mum, I need you to listen to me. There's some bad men out there that want to hurt us."

"But why?"

"There's no time to explain, Mum. I need you to follow me. We're going out onto the fire escape and I'll find us somewhere safe," said Tyler, although he couldn't think where. His mind raced with the words of John Cooper. "Your slippers are there by your feet. I have your pills and some clothes. Let's get out of here and we can talk about it when we're safe. Okay?"

"Oh," she said. It was the start of a panic attack. Tyler had witnessed many of her panic attacks begin with that word.

"No time to worry, Mum," he reassured her. "Let's go. It'll be like an adventure, okay?"

Tyler took his mother's hand and led her from the bedroom just as the front door began to pound.

"Quick, Mum, in here," said Tyler, leading his mum into the rear bedroom, which was too small for anything other than storing boxes, but the window opened onto the iron fire escape, which led to the ground floor alleyway that ran behind the buildings.

"Out there?" she said. "I can't go out there like this."

"Mum, please," said Tyler. "Please just do as I ask."

He forced the window open, which required a particular knack he'd learned as a child when he'd sneak out late at night to meet his friends.

The pounding on the door stopped, allowing for a moment of peace.

"Come on, Mum," he whispered, and held his hand out to help her through the gap.

She sat on the window ledge and swung her legs over until the brisk, cold wind lifted the edge of her dressing gown.

"Oh, Tyler, it's freezing," she said.

"I know, Mum. But not for long, I promise," he said, as the front door boomed with the shoulder of a man trying to get inside.

Tyler climbed through after his mum and leaned inside to grab the bag, just as he heard the front door explode open and a man stumble inside, followed immediately by two rough angry voices.

"Go down," whispered Tyler to his mum, as he pulled on the window to close it behind them. The men wouldn't know how to open it, which would give Tyler a head start.

Heavy footsteps on the lounge floor approached the tiny room. Just as the shape of the first man became silhouetted in the doorway, the window gave and slid shut with a click.

With the hard rain hitting his face, Tyler stepped back as the man pressed against the window, struggling to see through the frosted, reinforced glass. The face appeared to smile as Tyler moved to the top of the stairs. He glanced down at his mum who was carefully placing her slippered feet on the slippery iron stairs and clinging to the wet, slick handrail. Tyler looked back. The face moved away from the glass, but Tyler's hope lasted a fraction of a second before a piece of furniture was hurled at the window. The reinforced mesh held the glass together, but it fractured; it wouldn't take long to break through.

Tyler edged down the stairs.

"That's it, Mum," he said. "You're doing great. Are you okay?"

His mother didn't answer.

Another crash of the furniture smashing through the window. This time, tiny pieces of glass rained down onto the iron platform and to the ground below. A hole had been made in the mesh, and the man began to hammer with something, trying to smash through to outside.

"Keep going, Mum," said Tyler, keeping his eyes on the window above.

A man's head poked through the hole, searching around in the darkness until he caught the movement of Tyler on the stairs. With reluctance, the man pulled his head back inside. The crunch of stones and glass beneath his feet told Tyler he'd reached the ground, but he dared not take his eyes off the window above.

"Are you okay, Mum?' he asked.

But she didn't reply.

"Mum?"

Tyler turned to find a handgun pointing in his face. The one John had called Jack was staring back at Tyler with his hand over his mum's mouth.

"Going somewhere?" he asked.

CHAPTER TWENTY-FOUR

"So you thought you'd do a runner, did you, Tyler?" said John. "After our agreement, that's most unprofessional."

"No, it wasn't like that," replied Tyler. His voice was muffled by the thick hood that had been pulled over his head.

"Oh? Jack tells me you were climbing down the fire escape, Tyler, in the rain with who he can only imagine is your mother. Jack, remove her hood, mate, and get her wrapped up in a blanket or something. We don't want her bleeding dying on us yet."

Jack carefully pulled the hood off the lady's head to reveal a pair of wide scared eyes behind a thin facade of steely resentment.

"Can you get her a chair or something?" asked Tyler. "She's sick. She's supposed to be in bed, resting."

John took three paces forward until he was just inches from Tyler. He had to reach up to grab the hood, but he caught it and tugged until it fell from Tyler's face.

"That's better. I like to look a man in the eye when he's upset me," said John, aware that Tyler was a full twelve inches taller than himself. "What's wrong with your dear old mum then? She looks fine to me. A bit cold maybe."

"She's sick. It's cancer," said Tyler. "Please. I said I'd do what you asked. Get her a chair before she falls."

John studied the frail lady who seemed half the size of her son but could easily have once been a strong woman. He nodded to Jack who slid a chair behind her legs.

"Take a seat, Mrs Thomson," said John, and offered his hand to help her lower herself into the chair. "Find a blanket, Jack."

"Thank you," said Tyler. "I appreciate it."

"It's nothing. Where were you going?" asked John.

"Your men came for us. I didn't know what else to do."

"What are you talking about?"

"When we spoke, in the pub, you said you'd..." Tyler swallowed to control his voice. "You said you'd hurt my mum if I didn't do what you said."

"Right. So?"

"So when your men came, I thought you'd come for us. I didn't see any other way."

"You didn't see any other way," repeated John. He pronounced the words with slow and clear pronunciation. "These men, did they tell you they worked for me, Tyler?"

"Well, no. But we didn't hang around to talk to them. I woke my mum up and got us out of there."

"And where exactly was you planning to go?"

Tyler hesitated.

"Tyler?" John urged. "Is there something you're not telling me?"

"No. I didn't have a plan. I just knew I had to get out. They were kicking the door in. What was I supposed to do?"

John began to pace. He stuffed his hands into his coat pockets and took five steps to his right, letting the wooden heel of his Italian shoes click on the concrete floor. The noise reverberated in the large space and the tiled walls toyed with the sound until it faded away to nothing.

"Did you manage to get a good look at these men?" asked John.

"Not really," said Tyler. "Well, one of them, but I only saw his face in the dark, like a silhouette."

"As it turns out," said John, "you did the right thing. You should give yourself a pat on the back, Tyler."

"I did? So why are we here? And where are we?"

"Look around you, Tyler."

The boy turned to let his eyes wash across the tiled walls and cubicles where animals had once queued for the slaughter. He stopped when he saw the punch bag and weight bench. A rack of dumbbells lay against the tiled wall and a mat covered an area ten metres by ten metres.

"It's not much right now, Tyler. But one day, Cooper's Gym will be big, you mark my words."

"What's with the tiled walls and the smell?"

"That, Tyler, is the smell of fear. Fear and death," said John. He watched as Tyler's face sank even further. "It was a slaughterhouse. I bought it a few years ago. It comes in handy for times like this, you know? Sometimes a man in my position needs to be able to hose the blood off the floor."

Tyler gave him a sideways glance.

"They were going to tear it down and build some new swanky apartments, but the locals were against it. They said the building is a part of Plaistow history. So I bought it and I gained a few loyal fans in doing so. It's always good to have the public on your side when you're in the spotlight, Tyler. That's a lesson you should learn if you're going to be on stage."

"On stage?"

"In the ring, Tyler. If the crowds are with you, cheering your name, you'll feel on top of the world. If they're not, you're just queuing for the slaughter."

"So who were those men, if they don't work for you?" asked Tyler.

John took the five steps back to stand in front of the huge but naive boy.

"Those men, Tyler, were the opposition. I don't know how they found out about you, but they obviously did, and tried to put you out of the game. It won't happen again."

"They were going to kill us?" asked Tyler.

"I don't know," replied John. "I doubt they'd kill you. But they'd hurt you enough so you couldn't fight."

Tyler looked down at his mum who had fallen asleep in the chair.

"She looks comfy," said John.

"It's the meds," replied Tyler. "Look, John, I said I'd fight for you. And I will. But she's really sick. Can we get her somewhere? She needs rest."

"And what about you?

"What about me?" asked Tyler.

"Do you need rest?"

"No," replied the boy. "I need to train. I can feel the energy inside me. I won't sleep until I've worked out."

"Jack?" called John.

"Yes, boss."

"Get Mrs Thomson to the flat above the pub. She can have the spare room." He turned to Tyler. "Is that alright for you?"

"She needs care," said Tyler.

"I'll make sure she's looked after."

"And her medication."

"Painkillers?" said John. "I presume they're in the bag."

Tyler nodded.

The double doors at the end of the room swung open with a crash and Mick walked in. He saw John talking quietly to Tyler and kept his distance. He'd been trained well. John turned his attention back to Tyler.

"Tyler, you have to understand one thing. I'm a businessman. I'm hard but fair. And you are a fighter who now works for me. It might seem like a rough deal, son, but if you win this fight for us, you'll be welcomed into this family and your poor old mum will want for nothing. You got that?"

Tyler nodded once more.

"Good. From now on, you train here. You eat here and you sleep here. You need to be on top form, son."

"What about my job?" said Tyler. "I'll be letting my boss down."

"You leave your boss to me. Give Mick his number and he'll take care of everything for you."

"He'll fire me. I was going onto the tools."

"Listen, Tyler. When you win this fight, you'll have more money than you know what to do with. Forget about your job. I'll have Mick take care of it for you. We'll tell your boss you're sick or something, you won't be coming back, and you're really sorry. We'll be convincing. That's something that Mick happens to be particularly good at."

"What about the old man? I'm supposed to train. I can't let him down."

"You leave the old man to me, Tyler. Stop worrying and focus on the fight. I've got a lot riding on you. I can't risk having you leave my sight."

"But who will train me? I need a trainer."

Tyler eyed John up and down and spent a little longer on the paunch John had been developing.

"My trainer. He's the best. He'll be here later. You do everything he says when he says it and you won't have any trouble. You deviate from his plan and you'll find yourself in hot water. Is that clear?"

"It's clear," replied Tyler, but his enthusiasm had plummeted.

"Don't worry about the old man and don't worry about the job. I told you. Leave them to me. I'll have someone swing by your flat and get you a bag of clothes."

"And my mum?" asked Tyler.

"Well, as nice as this place is, Tyler, it's really not accommodating enough for the likes of your lovely old lady. She'll be staying at my pub in the flat upstairs. It's lovely. I'll see to it that the girls behind the bar pop up and see her to make sure she's okay. Poor old girl could probably do with a drink, couldn't she?"

Tyler managed a weak smile at John's attempt to finish on a high, positive note.

"Go say goodbye to her," said John. "If you play your cards right, Tyler, the next time you see her, you'll have cash in your pocket and a smile on your face."

A curt nod at Mick summoned John's number two while Tyler settled next to his mum and reassured her that everything would be okay.

"How did you get on with Dixon's boy?" asked John.

"He's a rock, John. No family. No weaknesses."

"He must have something. Keep looking," said John. "What about the old man?"

"I sent Nobby and Jack round to sort him out."

"Good. The last thing we need is that nosy old bastard sticking his two pennies worth in. He's well connected and could be a lot of trouble for us."

"Oh, he won't be any trouble, John."

"You sound sure of yourself, Mick."

"I just drove past his gym on the way back from south of the water. They torched the place with him inside. He won't be sticking his two pennies in anywhere ever again, John."

CHAPTER TWENTY-FIVE

Although the flames had been extinguished, huge, thick plumes of black smoke billowed from the charred remains of the gym and the tyre shop that occupied the arch beside it.

Harvey stood in the shadows across the road and watched as the firemen began to roll the hoses into neat stackable rolls, and the last of the ambulances waited with open doors. A window of light in the darkness. Its counterpart had sped off twenty minutes previously just as Harvey had arrived on the scene.

A few junior police had cordoned off the road and senior officers spoke with senior firemen, presumably discussing probable cause and managing the scene of the crime. If it was indeed a crime. Harvey had no doubt the fire was the result of arson.

As the final gurney rolled unhurried towards the waiting ambulance, Harvey felt a stab of guilt and loss. The sheet that covered the huge corpse differentiated its load as a body and not a survivor with an oxygen mask over their face. The sheet, much the same as the one that had covered Harvey's sister all those years before, was not blood soaked like they were in the movies. In Harvey's experience, they rarely were. A blood-soaked sheet would indicate a pumping heart.

But there was no way anybody could have survived the hellish blaze that Harvey had witnessed. The size of the body beneath the sheet was unmistakable.

Harvey watched as the two paramedics struggled to load the heavy gurney into the ambulance then secured it in place. The driver called through on his radio to the hospital.

"Male. One hundred and thirty-five kilos. Dead on arrival."

A crackle of radio returned as the doors slammed. Harvey edged back into the shadows, stumbled against the wall and took three deep breaths.

For the second time in Harvey's life, he'd failed a Saville.

Another car door slammed close by and men's voices grew louder, rousing Harvey from his thoughts. He stepped back further into the shadows, but his boot nudged a discarded glass bottle, sending it rolling. The chink of glass against concrete was loud in the quiet alley.

The voices stopped as if the bottle had caught their attention. Harvey checked his exit, glanced back at the ambulance one last time, turned, and ran through the series of alleys to where he'd parked Melody's car.

The doorway of a corner shop provided a place to hide and check to see if he'd been followed. He waited a full minute then walked calmly to the car.

The rain had cleansed the street but the nearby fire had tainted the air as far as three streets away. Harvey took the back streets through Poplar, passing old pubs and gambling houses his foster father used to own. But none of them brought back fond memories. They had been violent times when Harvey was only ever called out to take care of someone, leave no trace, and then crawl back to his little house. Each time, it was as if he paused his own existence while people searched for the missing man, retaliated, and then carried on with life.

Tyler's flat looked very different in the half-light of dawn. A corner shop was opening up a few doors down, its owner heaving in the bundles of newspapers. The highway at the end of the road was growing busier and soon London would be a hive of activity. Harvey turned and gave Tyler's flat another pass, checking the parked cars as Julios would have him do. The sentiment seemed like the right thing to do and Harvey couldn't shake his mentor's words from his mind.

He parked five cars down from the entrance to Tyler's flat and sat with his hands on the wheel, questioning what he was doing. He was just some kid who said he was Julios' son. But with no real proof. If he'd meant that much, surely Julios would have said something.

But he wouldn't have.

The line in the sand was never crossed. It was part of who Julios had been. And Julios was gone. So the only person left to look out for his son was Harvey. He couldn't walk away. He had to know if it was true, if it really was him in the fire.

He found the ground floor entrance to the flat. The door was broken as if it had been forced. Harvey slipped inside and took the single set of stairs to the first floor where he saw two doors.

The first one, on the right-hand side, was adorned with religious beads and had the spicy smell of curry emanating from inside. The second door had been smashed off its hinges and was laying on the floor inside the flat. On the wall in the hallway inside, three photo frames took pride of place, as if they were memories that welcomed Tyler home each time he walked through the door.

The first was of Tyler and who Harvey assumed to be his mum. The second was an image of a much younger Tyler leaning on the ropes of a boxing ring. The third caught Harvey off-guard. Standing with a baby in his arms, and wearing his trademark three-quarter length leather jacket, was Julios.

A man's voice came from inside the flat, dull and monotone. Harvey unsheathed his knife from his back pocket and traced the voice to a small room at the back of the flat. A cold breeze flowed through as if a window was open. Apart from the broken door, there were no signs of struggle or robbery.

A large crash sounded from the same bedroom as the voice, loud but muffled. Harvey crept across the threadbare carpet and peered inside to find a man in a dark green bomber jacket smashing a small chest of drawers into the frosted, reinforced window. With the knife held by his side, Harvey watched as the man leaned through the hole he'd made and called down to someone.

Harvey stepped into the room.

But as he did, a blow from behind slammed into his lower back, sending a wave of dull, agonising pain through his body. With no time to turn and defend himself against a follow-up attack, he dropped to the floor and kicked out at his attacker's legs. It was a move Julios had taught him. The natural reaction for someone being attacked from behind is to turn and face the attack. But to drop to the ground out of harm's way and smash the man's knee was nearly always unexpected and extremely effective. His attacker fell to the floor behind Harvey, who rolled, swiped the blade cross the inside of the man's thigh, and then stood with his heavy boot held hard down on the man's throat as he began to bleed to death.

The first man pulled back into the room and reached inside his jacket for a gun. But Harvey was faster. With his boot firmly in place and resisting the struggles of the dying man, Harvey put his blade against the first man's neck.

"Don't move," said Harvey.

The man froze. "Who are you?" he said, clearly angered but controlling his voice.

"Listen carefully," said Harvey. He increased the pressure of his boot on the dying man's throat, which raised his heart rate. The pool of blood between his legs grew wider, spilling out in heavy spurts from his femoral artery. They could hear the gargled chokes of the dying man taking his last breaths. "Do you hear that?"

"I hear it," replied the man with the knife to his throat. He glanced down as his friend's body twitched for the final time and was still.

"What are you doing here?" asked Harvey.

"Looking for someone."

"Who?"

"A friend," the man replied.

Keeping his eyes on the man, Harvey gestured with a nod of his head at a framed photo on the floor, which must have been on top of the furniture he'd used to smash the window.

"Him?"

The man glanced down at the photo and nodded, being careful not to move his neck.

"Yeah, him," he replied.

"I just watched his body being dragged out of a fire," said Harvey. "And now I find you in his flat. Tell me why I shouldn't cut your throat right here, right now."

The man's eyes watered. He kept his cool, but Harvey saw the fear building inside.

"Who are you working for?"

"Why should I tell you that?" the man answered.

"Because I just killed your friend here in less than two seconds and I'd like to see if I can kill you faster."

"Dixon," replied the man with no hesitation. "Del Dixon."

"Take me to him."

CHAPTER TWENTY-SIX

Left to his own devices, Tyler sat on the end of the bench press that John had provided. He let his head drop into his hands and fought back the hot tears that reddened his eyes. Ahead of him, thirty metres away at the far side of the room, the two double doors invited him to leave. But his fight had gone. While John Cooper had his mum holed up, he needed to do everything he could to get her back safe.

His fat fingers covered his face, but he opened his eyes and stared at the doors, then exhaled, long and slow.

"You can make a try for them if you want," said a voice.

Tyler looked up. His eyes were foggy but allowed him to focus on a man of average build standing a few feet away.

"The doors," he said. "You can make a run for it if you want."

"What's the point?" replied Tyler, and he let his head fall back into his hands.

"So stop thinking about it."

"How would you know what I'm thinking about?"

"Intuition," the man replied in a whisper.

"Where did you even come from?" asked Tyler. "I didn't hear-"

"How could you have heard me?" the man replied. "You were too busy listening to the demons in your head argue over running for the doors or killing yourself."

"I wasn't thinking about that," said Tyler.

"You will be when I'm finished with you."

Before Tyler could respond, a hammer-like punch caught him on the side of his jaw, knocking him from the bench to the mat, where he rolled to his knees and held his face, working his jaw to test for damage.

"What the-"

A kick to his gut doubled him over and he rolled to his side sucking in air.

"Get up," said the man. The order wasn't barked or shouted. There was no emotion whatsoever in the words.

"Who are you?" asked Tyler, as he scrambled across the floor away from the man.

"You haven't earned my name yet," the man replied. "Come on. Fight me."

Pulling himself to his feet, Tyler straightened. But he wasn't ready for the three-punch combo to his kidneys. A crippling back-ache set in with immediate effect. Tyler tried to walk it off with his hands on his kidneys and his spine arched back, but another blow came from nowhere. The man's fist connected with the side of Tyler's head, rocking his vision into a dizzying swirl of white tiles and early morning sunlight beaming through the frosted windows high on the walls.

He dropped to his knees then fell to his side and assumed the foetal position, waiting for the world around him to stop spinning.

Not a sound was made by the man's feet, but Tyler heard him from the far side of the room, talking on his phone.

"You've got yourself a dead boy, John."

Tyler closed his eyes. A wave of nausea flowed through him and hung at the back of his throat, threatening to advance if he moved even a finger.

"No. There's no fight in him. He might be big, but he's soft," the man continued to say.

But Tyler pushed his voice away and tiny roots pushed through the shells of the seeds of suicide the man had planted. It was the only way out. They wouldn't hurt his mum if he was dead. She'd be taken into care.

"He wants to talk to you," said the man.

Tyler opened his eyes to find the man standing beside where he was laying, holding out a mobile phone. He hadn't made a sound. The man hit loudspeaker and held the phone at arm's length.

"Tyler?" It was John's voice. "Answer me, son. You're testing my patience."

"I'm here," said Tyler. He heard how weak his own voice sounded.

"You need to fight, son. If you can't fight, you're no good to me. And you know what happens if you're no good to me?"

Tyler let the words play over in his mind, but couldn't respond without releasing the damn that held back his tears.

"You disappear, Tyler," John continued. "You just vanish like you never existed. And your mum? Well, I haven't made up my mind yet. But you can guarantee the last few days of her life will be spent laying on her back earning all the money I've wasted on her sorry, waste-of-space son."

The heat behind Tyler's eyes drained to his face, sending a tingle of rage across Tyler's skin. He felt his cheeks tighten. His eyes pulsed once as his heart fed a shot of adrenalin into his bloodstream.

"Don't you dare lay a finger on her."

"You don't call the shots, Tyler."

He got to his knees.

"Here we go," said the man who held the phone.

"You know what I'm going to do, Tyler? Just to make sure you know I'm a man of my word. I've took your mum's medication and hid it. How long before she starts to really hurt?"

"That wasn't the deal," said Tyler.

"So fight," replied John. "There's a man standing in front of you.

He's half your size, a third of your weight, and he's ready to slap you around the room. He's one of the toughest men I know. He's going to put the phone on the bench. If you can put him down long enough to hit redial, I'll give your poor old lady a dose of painkillers. If not, she suffers until you fight like a man and beat him. Each time you beat him and call me, your mum gets a painkiller. The next call I receive will either be from you asking politely for me to ease your mum's pain, or it will be from my friend telling me you haven't grown a pair of balls big enough for your mum to deserve a painkiller, and that she deserves to suffer."

The call disconnected.

Tyler studied the man who turned his back and walked to the bench to place the phone down in clear sight. With casual indifference, the man stood opposite Tyler. He bounced a few times on the balls of his feet and threw a rapid combination of punches into the air before eying Tyler.

"I imagine, right now, your poor old mum is locked in a padded room with a bucket to piss in and only the memories of her dead son to keep her company," he said.

The thought of his mum lying in a strange room, sweating and clawing at her skin, washed over Tyler's mind.

'Control it,' Harvey's words whispered.

But Tyler's mind focused on his mother's anguished face, wrinkled with agony and suffering.

"How's she going to feel when she learns her own son wasn't man enough to come to her rescue?" said the man. His taunts faded to a monotonous, heartless whisper.

Through eyes blurred by tears, Tyler focused on the callous and cruel grin that beamed from the man's face, bearing yellowed teeth, broken and stained. Tyler felt rather than heard the rasp of the growl that emerged from his throat, its rhythm in perfect time with the blood that pulsed behind his eyes.

'Use it,' said Harvey.

And the man came for him.

CHAPTER TWENTY-SEVEN

"What do you mean you bloody killed him?" said John, sitting forwards in his chair and gripping the edge of his desk. "I didn't tell you to kill the bloke, did I? No, I did not. Oh, Jesus. We're going to have the whole bleeding who's who of East bleeding London on my bleeding doorstep, and let me tell you something, Mick, it will not be me that takes the rap for it. I've got a lot riding on this fight tomorrow night and what I don't need right now is enemies. Opponents, yes. Dixon is an opponent. But when you kill someone like Old Man McGee, you might as well go round to the neighbourhood villain's house, wake them up, spit in their tea, and jump into bed with their wife, Jack. Do you understand the gravity of the situation?"

With both hands flat on his desk, John splayed his fingers and could feel the sweat from the antique desk's fine leather inlay warming his hands.

"Mick said to go and sort him out," said Jack, and glanced across to Nobby for support.

"That's right, John," said Nobby. "He didn't tell us not to kill him."

It was too much for John.

"Jack, pour me a drink, will you?" said John. He pinched the bridge of his nose to try and stem the headache that was forming. "Tomorrow night, I have got every villain worth his salt in London coming to watch my number one fighter take on Mackie in a fight to the death. It just so happens that my boy was being trained by the old man himself and now he suddenly trains with me the day after the old man gets bleeding offed. These villains, Nobby, are not like you, mate. Oh, no. They're intelligent men. That's why they're good at what they do, and that's how they manage to stay out of prison."

He took a sip of the brandy Jack had placed on the desk and pulled a tissue from a nearby box to wipe the ring mark from the leather.

"Another trait of these men, Nobby, is that they are extremely dangerous and not men that I want as enemies. Especially when I've invited them into my bleeding pub to watch the fight."

"Can't we just deny it?" asked Jack.

"Deny it, Jack?" A pulse of tension washed across John's temple. "And how the hell am I supposed to do that when I've got the old man's best fighter working for me? I'll be bleeding slaughtered."

He stopped, put his glass down on the wooden coaster beside his desk phone, and tried to make sense of the ideas that ran amok in his mind.

"Is that what this is about?" he asked. "Are you two trying to have me taken out? Is this some ploy to land me in hot water because I can assure you if it is-"

"No, John. I swear," said Nobby.

"I didn't ask you to talk. Shut up," said John. Then he calmed. "Let me finish. It makes perfect sense. You get the entire community of villains to outcast me and you both get to go and work for who you want. Who is it? Who's contacted you?"

"No-one, John," said Jack. "Honest. We haven't been anything but loyal. I've been with you from the start."

"I know you've been with me a long time, Jack. That's how I

know your two weaknesses. The slightest sniff of a pair of panties or the alluring waft of banknotes and you're away with the fairies."

"We're not trying to set you up," said Nobby. His voice had calmed and he spoke with reason and without fear. "Mick told us to go and make sure the old man doesn't stick his nose into the fight, being that he was training the boy. So we went down there, to his gym-"

"Okay," said John. He sat back in his chair with his glass, admiring the way Nobby was handling the situation and wasn't falling to bits like Jack. "And did you talk to the old man?"

"No, he was out the back."

"So who did you speak to?"

"Some big fella. Black as they come, he was, and with a voice like a trombone."

"Lloyd?" asked John.

"That's it. Do you know him?"

"Everyone knows Lloyd, Nobby. He's the old man's able-bodied partner, and he's just as well connected as the old man. He comes from a family of drugged-up yardies in Bow. He's the only one in the family that doesn't crush scrap cars for a living, and he was one of the old man's first success stories until the booze and the pills got him."

"He's an alcoholic?"

"Que sera sera, Nobby," said John, and took a sip of his brandy.

"Right," said Nobby. "Anyway, he told us where to go, you know? Didn't want us around and made it very clear we weren't welcome there."

"And then what?"

"Well, what would you do if someone insulted you, John? What did you expect us to do?"

"You torched the place?"

"Just the front door, but I guess the rest of the place just took off."

"And what did you do?"

"Nothing we could do, John. It was out of control in seconds."

"You ran?"

Nobby answered the question with raised eyebrows and tight lips, and he held John's stare, aware of the immorality.

"Well, at least you're honest, Nobby. Bleeding stupid, but honest."

"So what do we do?" asked Jack. His voice was still trembling and stained with panic.

"What you two pair of clowns have done is start a war, Jack. There's going to be fifty of London's most fearsome gangsters in this pub tomorrow night and each and every one of them was friends with the old man, and that's not to mention the family of angry yardies that will be kicking doors in looking for an answer to who killed their brother. And right now, all roads lead to the Golden Ring. So in answer to your question, Jack, we prepare for the worst, and you better get your backside out on the street and make it right."

"How are we-"

"Just listen, Jack," said John. He sank the remainder of his brandy and slammed the tumbler back down on the wooden coaster. "I want you to do exactly what I say. If you cock this up, everything I've worked for is going to come crashing down, and it'll bury us alive."

CHAPTER TWENTY-EIGHT

In an old power station in the heart of South London in the shadow of towering, concrete blocks of flats, and surrounded by pockets of small, green parks and old office buildings, a make-shift boxing ring had been put together.

Years of damp had tainted the stale air. It was flavoured by a history of under-paid union worker's sweat, thick grease and heavy, iron machinery that had long since been sold for its scrap value, or reconditioned and sold to the highest bidding emerging market.

The rhythmic grunts of the two men in the ring echoed off the bare, Victorian, brick walls, accompanied only by the dull thuds of gloves on pads and the gruff, angry voice of a man in a sheepskin jacket and thick tortoise-shell glasses who leaned over the ropes, shouting at the larger of the two boxers. The bigger man sent a perfect hook through a poor defence, stunning the smaller boy, who rocked forwards then back.

"Don't just bleeding stand there, Mackie, you big girl," he shouted. "When you hit someone that hard, you follow up with more. Put him on his arse and don't let him up."

The man Harvey had found at Tyler's flat entered through the small side door and put his hand on Harvey's arm. It was a move Harvey presumed was designed to inform his boss that Harvey had been forced to accompany him, as opposed to the truth of the matter, that Harvey forced the man to lead him there and into the jaws of death.

The hand was removed moments after Harvey had delivered a silent glare, and the two men walked towards the ring. They stopped behind Del Dixon with room enough to watch the sparring.

"That's it, Mackie. Get in there," the older man shouted, his enthusiasm fully supported by the ropes. A cigar was lodged between two of his fingers while the others gripped the rope. Both hands were adorned with an array of sovereigns, signets, five-row keeper rings and a heavy gold watch that rested on his angled wrist. "Now take him down and keep him down."

Spittle shot from the man's mouth and his cigar waved in the air as the larger of the two fighters took the advantage on his opponent who stood swaying in the centre of the ring. He delivered a wild but powerful hook that lifted the boy's feet from the ring floor, causing him to land in an unceremonious heap with blood leaking from his mouth.

But the fight wasn't over. Harvey expected Dixon to give his fighter a pat on the back and turn to see Harvey. But instead, Dixon leaned further into the ring.

"Now, Mackie, don't let him wake up, son."

The fighter was standing over his opponent, a tentative look of fear etched onto his young face as he locked eyes with Dixon, who leaned further into the ring.

"Finish him, you big dumb bastard," he screamed. "If you don't finish that boy, I'll wake him up myself and let him give you what for."

The veins on Dixon's temple were visible even from the distance of a few metres away, where Harvey stood.

The boy looked down at his opponent, whose eyes flickered once and whose arms began to move.

"Now, Mackie," screamed Dixon.

Mackie dropped to his knees beside the younger boy and placed his hand on his opponent's head as if to offer a silent apology.

"Mackie," screamed Dixon again, his voice rising several octaves.

It took Mackie three hard punches to the boy's head before the crack of bone could be heard.

"That's it," said Dixon, his voice quieter. "You've done the worst of it. Send him on his way."

Mackie hovered above the dying boy as a pool of blood began to form by his knees. Then he brought his arm up for one final blow, raising it high above his head, clenching his gloveless fist and, with his eyes focused on the side of the boy's head, he delivered the fatal blow.

The crack of bones and grunt of Mackie's exertion echoed in the vast room, but the sound faded as fast as the boy's life. Mackie wiped the blood spatter from his face with his forearm and fell across the body at his knees. The man beside Harvey turned away and exhaled, long and slow.

Dixon nodded his approval, then straightened.

"Good lad," he said, and took a long pull on his cigar. The ember crackled amid the smoke that swallowed Dixon's wrinkled face. "It gets easier, Mackie. The more you do it, the easier it gets. Now get yourself washed up and go for a run. One more tonight then tomorrow is the big day."

Dixon stepped down to the concrete floor using the three ropes for handholds and with his teeth clenching the cigar butt between his thin lips. Then he wiped his hands on a towel that was draped over the lowest rope and tossed it into the ring, catching sight of Harvey and the man beside him as he did.

Dixon's head cocked inquisitively, and with a subconscious habit, he pushed his thick glasses onto his nose before retrieving his cigar. The soles of his brogues clicked on the concrete floor as he took five steps towards Harvey. His right hand found the fat sovereign on his left and turned it a full circle before positioning the coin flat on his fist as if he was readying for a punch using his rings for maximum results with minimum damage to his hands.

Then, as if asking a question, he searched from his man to Harvey and back again, finally resting on Harvey with magnified cold eyes, tinted brown by the lenses of his thick-framed glasses. He took a final, long pull on his cigar, tilted his head back and blew the smoke above him, where it was lost to the dank, stale air.

Finally, he tossed the remains of his cigar to the floor, crushed the ember with the heel of his shoe, and placed his hands inside the deep pockets of his sheepskin jacket.

"Who the bleeding hell are you?"

CHAPTER TWENTY-NINE

The first punch connected with Tyler's nose, smarting his eyes. The second found his kidney, followed by a third that broke through Tyler's guard and glanced off his brow. In an instant, the warm sting of blood found the corner of his eye. Tyler jumped back, maintaining his guard, and worked the mix of tears and blood from his sight with rapid blinks of his eye.

"Can you see her, Tyler?" said the man. "Can you see her doubled over in pain, clawing at the door for someone to help?"

Tyler launched an attack. A quick succession of body blows were all blocked, and a final hook to the man's head fell short by a whisker as he dodged back.

"But there's no-one to help her, Tyler," he continued.

Then the man dodged and weaved a series of head blows. The final jab connected square on and sent him reeling back. But he recovered and came at Tyler with a relentless succession of kicks and punches that forced Tyler back against the tiled cubicle where, long ago, livestock would have been dragged and bolted and strung up to drain.

No matter where Tyler guarded, the blows landed elsewhere.

Rock hard fists, delivered with precision and power, slammed into Tyler's body with tiresome energy, until the man was so absorbed in his rhythm and breathing that he got close enough for Tyler to open his arms wide and smash his massive forehead into the man's face.

He stumbled back, but the reprisal was brief. Within two seconds, he was ready to fight again, his mouth running with blood.

"Is that it, Tyler? Your poor old mum is banging on the door, begging for help, and all you can do is stand in the corner and take a beating."

Tyler shoved off the wall.

"They'll need to tie her down. You know that?"

With his shoulder set, Tyler charged at the man, but he side-stepped and delivered a kick to the back of Tyler's head.

"They'll be so bored of listening to her sobs and screams, she'll be gagged and tied to the bed."

Tyler charged again, but this time, the man didn't side-step. He stood his ground, coiled and greeted the charge with a powerful uppercut that rocked Tyler's brain. Tyler stumbled then dropped to a knee to steady himself.

'Control it,' Harvey's calm voice came to him.

He ducked a sidekick. The man's leg passed over his head and Tyler reached up, catching it in the crook of his left arm. Instinct took over and he stood, kicking out at the man's legs and sweeping him off his remaining foot.

The man went down but Tyler still had his leg. He began to twist, fending off futile kicks until the man rolled with the twist and lay on his front. Tyler placed a huge foot on the back of his neck and bent his leg up towards his head until the man's body arched to its maximum stretch.

Three slaps of the man's hand on the floor and Tyler released him. He turned and walked towards the bench where the phone lay waiting. His mum would be suffering just a call away.

"Where do you think you're going, big fella?"

Tyler stopped and turned, and a hard jab found its mark on his face.

"You haven't earned that yet."

"I got you down," said Tyler, blinking away the throb of the punch.

"And I got back up again," the man replied. "If you want to survive this fight, you'll need to do better than that."

The man's smaller size seemed to have no bearing on his confidence. He began to dance around, hopping from foot to foot.

Tyler raised his guard.

"Jerry," said the man, and offered Tyler a smile.

"Jerry?" replied Tyler. He planted his feet and met the man's eyes while his brain focused on his arms and legs.

"My name," the man replied. "That's all you earned. I was told you can fight, but all I've seen so far is a big, muscle-head cry-baby who misses his mum. This time, we fight for real. No tapping out. No going easy. I want you to hurt me. I want you to pick up that phone with pride and tell John Cooper to feed your mum those painkillers. So hit me."

Tyler didn't move.

"I said hit me, you big dumb idiot."

'Use it.'

"Fight me," said Jerry. His smug face dropped as frustration set in. "Hit me. Or I'll call John myself and tell him to strip your mum naked and send the boys into her room."

'Control it.'

"Are you retarded? Hit me."

'Use it.'

The first jab was easily dodged with a duck of Tyler's head and he responded with a hook that found Jerry's jaw. But the punch hadn't perturbed Tyler's aggressor. He retaliated with a hook that Tyler ducked back to avoid, then delivered his own that found its mark.

Seeming to take delight in the volley of punches, Jerry launched into a frenzy of failed attacks with Tyler managing to duck or block each one with a new-found calm composure. The few hits that he did take didn't hurt but only seemed to strengthen his resolve. Even when Jerry slipped a few wild kicks at Tyler, he absorbed them and replied with his own, which were more powerful.

The volley grew in intensity when Jerry's punch cracked Tyler's jaw. Moments later, Tyler smashed Jerry's nose and the two men entered into a rhythm of punches and kicks, neither blocking nor dodging but matching each other one for one.

The only difference between the two men was that with each blow Tyler landed, the control over Jerry's rage weakened and each punch he replied with grew in anger. But Tyler had found a state of emotionless calm. He could read Jerry's next move by watching the way his body leaned or catching the flick of his eye to its target. Jerry's rage grew to a point where he dropped his guard to coil for a punch. Tyler's hand shot out, grabbing his throat and squeezing hard.

Jerry fought back. The volley was over and he pounded Tyler with both arms, each punch easily absorbed with the resilience of a rock. Tyler tensed, gripped harder than before and lifted Jerry from his feet. The punches turned to kicks as Jerry tried to pry Tyler's hands from his throat, lashing out at whatever target his feet could find.

But it was too late. Tyler's left hand found the waistband of Jerry's loose sweatpants. He took a long deep breath, then raised the smaller man above his head, kicking and flailing.

A stream of abuse aimed at Tyler's mother began to run free from Jerry's spiteful mouth, but the sound was a distant noise, irrelevant and unfathomable.

'Use it.'

Tyler arched his back, sending all the energy he could muster into his huge, broad shoulders, then with the power coursing through his body, he slammed Jerry down onto the hard, concrete floor.

CHAPTER THIRTY

"Take her pain away," said the voice on the other end of the phone.

John recognised the number, but the confidence in the voice was new.

"I knew you had it in you, Tyler."

"I want to talk to her."

"All in good time," said John.

"I want her taken care of."

"You're in no position to make demands, Tyler. I told you to trust me. Do you?"

"You have to earn trust," replied Tyler.

"How ready are you?" asked John, leading the conversation towards the big fight.

"My mother, look after her or I won't be fighting."

The call disconnected. The doors of the pub opened up onto a cold and miserable morning. A car drove past with a swish as its tyres cut through the surface of water and the car's rear lights reflected, fragmented and multiplied in the road.

John stepped across the street, mindful of ruining his shoes in the deep water, then turned and looked back at the Golden Ring. The building was symmetrical with two windows, a door, and a patch of mismatched brickwork that betrayed the old off-license window, where the landlord would have served thirsty customers during the forced out-of-hours periods. The window had been bricked up long before John had taken on the pub.

The lights on the top floor of the house were all off, except for John's office at the front and the small spare bedroom at the back where the boy's mum was likely lying in a pool of her own pain-filled tears. He'd ask one the staff to take her a painkiller when they arrived.

The car park to the right-hand side of the old building was empty. John's Range Rover was parked around the back behind locked gates. He pictured how it might look that evening. Instead of the usual vans, hatchbacks and boring, cheap family wagons, the car park would be filled with the finest selection of cars that ever graced its tarmac. Tonight would be the night to forge alliances. Nothing formal, but a display of wealth and power would go a long way with the men that he'd invited. When the time was right, he'd have men to call upon. Behind the scenes and buried in the facades of conversation, the evening would host a plethora of back scratching. The time to stand out was now. The time to be recognised was now. The time to sow the seeds that would see John rise up was now.

The night needed to go without a hitch.

The headlights of an approaching car turned into the road a few hundred yards away. In the dawn light, John couldn't make out the model so he stepped back out of sight until it reached him, slowed then pulled into the car park. Mick climbed out carrying two coffees in takeaway cups. He shut the door with his foot and hit the fob to lock the car. The indicators flashed once and the interior light faded to nothing. Mick was John's best man. He was reliable, loyal, and as tough as they come. Plus, he had brains, a trait that rarely went hand in hand with brawn.

Keeping to the shadows, John watched as Mick approached the pub with furtive glances at his surroundings. He saw John, checked the street both ways, and crossed over to join him, handing him a coffee. Mick let a few seconds pass before speaking, apparently gauging John's mood at Nobby and Jack's cock-up.

"Big night tonight, John," he said.

"It'll be big alright, Mick."

"I heard about Nobby and Jack," said Mick. "I didn't give the order, but I take responsibility. I obviously wasn't clear enough."

John glanced to his side. Mick was looking at the pub, his face strong. His eyes showed no sign of fear.

"Jack's a liability, Mick," replied John. "Even if we get through this tonight, he'll still be a problem."

Knowing that Mick would understand the underlying tones and find a way of getting rid of Jack, John turned back to look at his pub, leaving Mick to ponder on a solution. He was good at solutions.

"Do you think the other firms will go for it?" asked Mick. "I mean, word from you would be one thing, but spreading a rumour that Dixon killed the old man, well, who would believe them?"

John smiled.

"That's the game, Mick. All this might even work in our favour and nothing pleases me more than profiting from disaster."

John took a sip of his coffee. The steam fogged his glasses. He licked his lips, cleared his throat, and let his lenses clear.

"If I were to contact the other firms," began John, "and tell them it was Dixon that had the old man taken out in an effort to upset my fighter enough to lose the fight, I would have to go to the top dogs. The big boys, Mick. And I would have to stand there and tell them a bare-faced lie. Should, in the yet unforeseen turn of events, it be discovered that it was indeed my boys that took him out, then that lie, alongside the murder of one of London's most-loved men would see me buried alive. Probably in the same hole as you, Nobby and Jack."

Mick nodded.

"However," said John, "if Jack and Nobby were to shoot their mouths off in a bar, and just happened to be overheard by some keen and green upstart that worked for one of the other firms, then if and when the time came for me to defend my position, I would have told no lies."

"You'd still be killed, John. We all would."

"With honour, Mick. With honour," replied John. "And with any luck, I'd be buried in a different hole to the fool."

Mick gave a small laugh and a short exhale through his nose, then took a long sip of his coffee.

"How do you think it'll play out?" asked Mick.

"They'll wait. The firms will want to see the fight. Everyone's talking about it, you know?"

"Yeah, I hear."

"They'll all have wagers. The Robinsons will have wagers with the McIntyres. The MacIntyres will have wagers with the West London firms. And the paddies will be balls deep with the lot of them. Nothing will happen until one of our boys is lying in a pool of his own blood. Pockets will be fuller, smiles will be wider and the bubbly will be flowing. That's when it'll happen, Mick."

Mick nodded his head in agreement. "We need to be ready."

It was John's turn to issue a half-hearted laugh. "Listen, Mick. If there's one thing I've learned in this game, it's that the man with the biggest pair of balls doesn't always win. Nor is it the man with the biggest brain on his shoulders. You need to have both. You need balls of steel and you need to be smarter than anyone else. You don't need to be a rocket scientist, just smarter than the men you're up against. Did you ever hear about the guys in Africa? One of them asks the other what he'd do if a lion came, and he said, run."

"You can't outrun a lion," said Mick.

"That's what the other guy said. And the first guy replied, I know, I'd just have to outrun you. That's the point, Mick, you don't need to be faster than the lion. You just need to be faster than the blokes you're with."

John took a sip of his coffee, pleased with his analogy, and let his glasses de-mist.

"So do you reckon the other firms will go for it then, John?" asked Mick. "Like I said, we need to be ready if they don't."

John smiled. It was a question he'd thought about all night, lying awake in bed listening to the crying of the boy's mum a few rooms away.

"If it happens, Mick, there'll be absolutely nothing we can do about it. It's too late to cancel now, and besides, it would make us look guilty. We'd need more than a hundred men, which we don't have. We'd need firepower, which we don't have enough of. And we'd need friends to get us out, which at this point, we wouldn't have at all. If they don't fall for it, and all fingers point at us, the best thing we can do is take it like men. I'm not going down like a coward, Mick. If it comes to it, I'll stand there and tell them all it was us, and tell them to do their worst. In years to come, they'll be talking about me with a degree of respect. If we run, we'll just be another firm that came and didn't have the balls to see it through."

CHAPTER THIRTY-ONE

"The way I see it, we both have a common enemy," said Harvey.

He walked beside Del Dixon along London's River Thames. Although Harvey had grown up in East London, the south side offered a far better view of the city that even he couldn't deny.

"So you want my help to get at John Cooper?" said Dixon. "You killed one of my men and walked into my manor, bold as brass, and you've got the audacity to ask for my help."

"It's *you* that needs *my* help," said Harvey. "And I killed a man who attacked me. It was him or me, and I'm not in the habit of asking who someone is before they slot me."

"Well, perhaps you bleeding well should next time," replied Dixon. "You don't know who you might upset."

Harvey didn't reply.

"What's he done to you anyway?" asked Dixon. "Why do you want to get at John Cooper?"

"Does it matter?" said Harvey. He stopped to lean on the iron handrail that ran alongside the pathway. The river flowed past, fast with the morning tide.

Dixon joined him and leaned on the railings. The body language wasn't threatening, but Harvey could see the older man trying to maintain the upper hand.

"As it happens, yes, it does matter," said Dixon. "When a man I never clapped eyes on before kills one of my best men, then forces the other one at knife point to bring him to me, it raises eyebrows. In particular, my eyebrows. Can you see them? My eyebrows. They're raised, are they not?"

Harvey gave him a brief glance, then turned back to the river.

"I'd say so," he said.

"Right. So when my eyebrows are raised," continued Dixon, "it is not a good sign for the man that raised them."

"So take care of me," said Harvey. "We're standing by the river. All it would take would be for you to shoot me and throw my body over the side. Why don't you?"

"Are you bleeding mental?" said Dixon. "You're either extremely stupid or extremely brave. Which is it?"

"Why don't you shoot me and throw me in the river?" said Harvey. "You'll soon know."

Dixon shook his head in disbelief.

"So?" said Dixon.

"So what?"

"So it does matter. It matters why you want to get at John Cooper. Of course it matters. Everything matters. For all I know, he sent you here."

"He killed a friend of mine," said Harvey.

"And who was your friend?"

"*That* doesn't matter," replied Harvey. "What matters is the fire he started last night."

"Fire? What fire?"

Harvey checked Dixon's expression with a sideways flick of his eyes. He genuinely wasn't aware of any fire.

"Well, if you don't know by now, I'm pretty sure you're about to find out," said Harvey.

"Don't play games with me, sunshine. You've pushed your luck too far already. What fire?"

"Do you know the gym in the arches in Poplar?"

"In Poplar?" said Dixon. "You mean Old Man McGee's place?"

Harvey didn't reply.

"He torched it? John Cooper? Are you sure?"

"It was either him or you, and your men were busy elsewhere."

"Why would he do that?" asked Dixon. "Why would he torch the old man's place?

"To get at my friend," said Harvey. "But if I were you, I wouldn't be concerned with why he did it. I'd be concerned with the ramifications."

"Explain," said Dixon. He pushed off the rail, planted his hands into his sheepskin jacket and pulled out a fresh cigar.

"Don't do that near me," said Harvey. "It stinks."

Dixon cut the end of his cigar, flicked open his Zippo lighter, and lit it.

"Like I said," said Dixon. "Explain."

"When I walked into your makeshift gym this morning, you were watching your fighter beat another boy to death."

"So?"

"So I happen to know that John Cooper is also preparing for a fight. It's not difficult to see that your boy is up against his boy, and judging by the mess your boy Mackie made, it's a fight to the death."

"So you're observant. Tell me about the ramifications."

"I haven't seen a prize fight like that for a long time. They stopped years ago," said Harvey.

"We reintroduced them," said Dixon. His smile spoke volumes about how much money the man had made.

"Bigger stakes," said Harvey. "Bigger stakes means bigger risks. I'm guessing that this isn't the first fight."

"There's been a few," replied Dixon.

"And if it's anything like how it used to be, John Cooper has been trying to get to your boy, and you've been trying to get John Cooper's boy. Hence why I found your men in his flat last night."

"Just get to the point," said Dixon, urging Harvey forward with his thoughts. Revealing the thought process piece by piece was Harvey's intentional way of seeing who Del Dixon really was. And with each word Harvey spoke, the man beside him grew tense and agitated.

"What would you do if your boy Mackie said he was out? If he said he wasn't going to fight for you?"

Dixon shrugged.

"You wouldn't just send him back to his old life to carry on as normal, would you?" said Harvey.

"Probably not, no," said Dixon.

"So what do you think Cooper would do if his boy told him he wasn't going to fight for him anymore?"

"The same as me, I guess."

"And what do you think John Cooper would do if, whilst he was taking care of the boy, he accidentally took care of Old Man McGee, who incidentally trains some of the best prize fighters in London, and who incidentally works for some of the biggest faces in the city?"

"How do you know about the old man? Who are you?"

"Who I am doesn't matter. But I've been around a long while, and the old man was the best trainer around even when I was a boy."

The slow realisation of Harvey's words took its place on Dixon's face. His cigar hand fell to his side and his eyes grew huge behind his thick glasses. He regained his composure and leaned on the rail beside Harvey again, but on the other side, so his cigar smoke was carried away by the wind.

"You think Cooper is trying to point the finger at me?"

"Like I said," said Harvey. "It's you that needs my help."

"And how, pray tell, do you plan on doing that? If what you just said is true, my photo will be pinned to every dartboard in every pub in London."

"How long have you got until the fight?" asked Harvey.

Dixon checked the heavy and expensive watch beneath the fur of his sheepskin cuff.

"Sixteen hours," he replied.

"Well," said Harvey, pushing off the rail and beginning the slow walk back the way they came, "I can't help you fight every face in town, but give me the day with Mackie, and I can make sure you beat John Cooper."

"What's in it for you?" asked Dixon. "What's your prize in this master-plan of yours?"

Harvey felt the familiar pang of retribution in his chest. He smiled and let it warm his veins.

"John Cooper," said Harvey. "John Cooper is my prize."

CHAPTER THIRTY-TWO

Breakfast consisted of eggs and bacon served up on a paper plate with a plastic knife and fork. It was wasn't the athlete's diet that Tyler had been hoping for, but having spent so much energy putting Jerry down, he devoured the food.

"Is he ready?" asked John, as if Tyler wasn't there.

Jerry nodded.

"He got through me twice," he replied.

"Good," said John. "So he's ready for the last part of his training then, is he?"

"The last part?" asked Tyler. He had envisaged a rest day before the fight. The other trainers all gave him rest days. But John ignored the question.

"He's ready," said Jerry. His eyes met Tyler's as he looked up from his plate of greasy bacon, but then looked away as if he was ashamed of admitting his defeat to John.

"What's the next part of the training?" asked Tyler. "I put Jerry down, twice now. I should be resting."

John span to face him.

"You should be doing what the bleeding hell I tell you to do.

When I say eat, you eat. When I say stand, you stand. And when I tell you to fight, you damn well fight. Do you understand me, son?"

The words hit Tyler hard. Putting Jerry down hadn't bought him any favours. There was no new display of respect. He pushed off the bench, stood and dropped the empty paper plate to the floor. John's face twisted. One of his eyes squinted and one side of his teeth showed. They were straight and clean, but yellowed with age.

"I didn't tell you to stand," said John.

Tyler didn't reply.

John poked his index finger into Tyler's chest.

"Did you hear me, boy? I didn't tell you to stand."

Being a full twelve inches above John, and well over twice as broad, Tyler felt the urge to flatten him.

'*Control it.*'

He stepped back half a pace, away from the offending finger, but didn't sit back down.

"What's the next part of the training?" he asked.

"Jerry," said John, "I think you've done it, my old mate. I think you've turned this soft piece of mushy turd into a man. Did you see that? Did you see the way he tried to defy me?" Closing the gap between himself and Tyler, John looked directly up at the huge boy. "I like the new Tyler. He's got balls," he said. Then his hand shot out and grabbed Tyler's crutch, squeezing hard, doubling Tyler over and sucking the breath from him.

"Now you listen to me, sunshine. Until the fight is over, you're mine. Do you understand me?" He increased the pressure.

Tyler nodded, but John's hand tightened even more.

"I said, do you understand me, Tyler?"

"Yes. Yes. I understand," said Tyler, and let out a long breath as he fought to control the pain. As he did, the pain seemed to ease. His anger hovered at the forefront of his mind, but clarity began to emerge through the fog. He saw images of what John's face would look like when he squeezed the life from him. He would wait for the right time.

'*Channel your emotions.*'

John released his grip on Tyler's groin.

"Good," he said. "Now sit down. I haven't finished with you yet."

Tyler dropped to the bench. It was the right thing to do. The time to destroy John Cooper wasn't yet, not until his mother was safe. Until then, he'd play the game. He'd fight, and if it took every last piece of him to win, he'd make sure he did.

"The last part of the training," began John, as he put his hands into his jacket pockets and paced back and forth, "will be a test of your resolve. It'll make or break you. But remember, if you break, your poor old mum breaks too."

The mention of his mum sent a pulse of rage through Tyler. The pulsing behind his eyes was a familiar sensation now, as was the warm release of adrenaline into his blood, which heightened the feeling in his fingers. He watched as John pulled his phone from his pocket, hit the redial button, and put the phone to his ear.

"Mick? Bring the boy. It's time to see if our Tyler has what it takes."

CHAPTER THIRTY-THREE

The sound of car doors slamming outside initiated a wave of activity. Jerry had been tending to Tyler's wounds. He washed the blood from his torn eyebrow, applied heat packs to his bruised ribs and cleaned the blood from Tyler's nose, making him ready for another fight.

John sat and watched. Jerry was a good ally to have. The man was as tough as they come and had been around fighters all his life. He'd originally been a pikey that had taken the East London prize fighting scene by storm. John had recognised his talent, but the man couldn't be trusted. He could be called upon to help with training, but he'd run off with whatever you left laying around unless the job was worth more than whatever he could take. Once a pikey, always a pikey.

The doors opened and Jack fell through, stumbling to the floor. He pushed himself up onto his elbow and looked around the place with wonder as Mick closed the doors behind him. Mick then bent down and grabbed hold of Jack's jacket collar. The room sang with the echoes of shouts, Jack's voice rising an octave at a time, until Mick hoisted him up and onto the canvas floor of the makeshift ring. Jack rolled beneath the lowest rope, not with the keen desire to fight, as some men would, but just to get away from Mick, who had left his mark on Jack's face while persuading him to climb into the boot of his BMW.

"What's all this then?" said Jack.

He looked for a way out of the ring, but each side was covered by Mick, Jerry and John. The fourth side wasn't covered, but even if he managed to climb out of the ring, he'd have to get past all three of them to reach the doors.

"There's no use in running, Jack," said John.

"But what have I done?" Jack replied. He was gripped by fear, exactly where John wanted him. "I did what you said, and they fell for it. Honest. Everyone's talking about how Dixon's boys torched the gym. We're in the clear."

"Maybe so, Jack," said John. "But what's next? Where do you go from here?"

"I don't understand, John. You said it was all okay. I did what you asked."

John waited a few seconds, enjoying the panicked reactions of Jack as he sought to distance himself from Mick and Jerry, who had closed in and stood by the ropes watching him with as much satisfaction as John. Mick's gratification stemmed from his loyalty to John and nothing more. Jerry's grin, which seemed to broaden with every passing moment, stemmed from his lust for violence and his passion for watching people suffer.

John glanced behind him to where Tyler sat on the bench with a towel around his shoulders staring up at Jack. John could almost see the cogs falling into place.

"Even if tonight goes without a hitch, Jack, even when it's all over and Dixon is broken and destitute, I'm still left with you, aren't I?"

"I've always been loyal, John."

"You've always been a liability, Jack, is what you've always been. What am I supposed to do? Set you free? What would you do? You're like a dog, Jack. One that's bitten too many people and is too long in the tooth to set free. You wouldn't survive, mate. You couldn't get a job. Who'd have you?"

"John, don't do this."

"It's too late, Jack. I thought long and hard about this. About what to do with you."

"John, I'd do anything. You know I would."

John continued, ignoring Jack's pleas, much to Jerry's visible delight.

"I know you're loyal, Jack. I know you wouldn't go running to some other firm, even if you could find one that would take you on."

"No, John, I wouldn't do that. That would be betraying you."

"So, Jack, I wondered, how can Jack show me one last time just how loyal he really is? What can he do to demonstrate how sorry he is for the monumental cock-up that could destroy me and everything I've worked for?"

"Just tell me, John."

"And that's when it hit me," said John. "It was a revelation. This moment of clarity. The answer to the problem of what to do with a man whose stupidity has defied all odds, but whose loyalty has beholden him to me."

John kept his eyes on Jack but called out behind him.

"Tyler," he said, "this is the last part of your training, son. Get in the ring."

"You want me to fight him?" said Tyler. He was standing beside the ring, confused at what was being asked of him.

John pulled his phone from his pocket again and held it in front of him as if he were revealing a jack of hearts from a deck and asking him to memorize the card.

"At the end of this phone, Tyler, is your poor old mum. Right now, she's locked inside a room. The painkillers will be wearing off and her bucket will be full of a foulness that I just can't even begin to imagine."

"You told me you'd take care of her."

"I told you I'd give her a painkiller if you got Jerry down. And you did. Now I'm telling you I'll give her more if you finish off our loyal friend."

"What do you mean finish?" asked Jack. But John ignored him.

"Get in the ring, Tyler," said John.

"I can't do that," said Tyler. "That's-"

"Then your poor old mum suffers. I'll be sure to call the girls and have them pass the message on, shall I?" said John. "I'll make sure your mum knows that while she fights the pain that courses through her fragile little body, her son here, who has the chance to put a stop to it all, refuses to. Because it's what?"

"It's immoral," said Tyler.

"Did you hear that, Mick?" said John. "Immoral. Shall I tell you what Jack here did to deserve it?"

"John, I fixed all that," said Jack from inside the ring.

"Shut it, Jack," said John. He returned his attention to Tyler. "How close was you to the old man?"

"Old Man McGee?" asked Tyler. "Not close, but I respect him. What do you mean, was? What's happened?"

John let a smile creep onto his otherwise emotionless face.

"It's quite a story," said John. "And, if you can see past the emotion, it's actually pretty funny. See, Mick told Jack here to make sure the old man didn't get involved in tonight's fight. We didn't want to mess up your training, and after all, at that point, you were doing us a favour."

"Right..." It was clear that Tyler knew where the story was going but let John carry on.

"But instead of having a word in his earhole, polite like, he managed to upset the big fella, the old man's sidekick and able-bodied bodyguard."

"Lloyd?" asked Tyler.

"That's right. You're catching on," said John. "Well, Jack being Jack, the hard man he is, didn't let nature run its course. He didn't let sleeping dogs lie. No, Tyler. He offed them. Both of them."

Tyler looked up at Jack, who saw the rage in Tyler's eyes.

"He didn't just kill them, Tyler. He burned them alive," said

John. "I don't think the old boy deserved that at all. He was, after all, a pillar of our society. But Jack thought he knew better."

"I didn't mean to-"

"So you see, Tyler," said John, overpowering Jack's whining pleas, "*Jack* needs a way of making amends. *You* need the training." He stopped and closed the distance between himself and the boy, placing his hand on Tyler's massive shoulder. "And your poor old mum needs her medication."

CHAPTER THIRTY-FOUR

"What makes you think you can teach me anything Del's trainer hasn't been able to?" asked Mackie. He bounced from foot to foot and shook his limbs, then threw a combination into the air as Harvey eased himself through the ropes. "Nobody even knows you."

"And that's the way it's going to stay," replied Harvey.

He slid his padded leather motorbike jacket from his shoulders and hung it over one of the corners. Mackie eyed his physique and seemed to grow in confidence. While Mackie bounced around, Harvey took three paces forward and stood in front of him, two arms' length away with his hands on his hips.

"Come at me," said Harvey.

As expected, Mackie led with his weak hand into a straight jab, followed by a hook with his right. Harvey ducked out of the jab and before the boy had regained his guard, Harvey's hand had shot up and grabbed his throat.

Mackie's eyes widened with fright. He tried to prise open Harvey's hands but Harvey was too strong. He threw three wild punches to Harvey's gut, all weak and using more oxygen than he had left in his lungs, leaving him in a panicked state. Harvey shoved Mackie backwards and he stumbled, falling to the canvas.

"What are you doing, you lunatic? You could have killed me," said Mackie, his voice high and his confidence levelled.

"My point exactly," replied Harvey.

"I hope you know what you're doing, Harvey," said Dixon from his place beside the ropes.

Harvey didn't reply.

"Well, don't just sit there, Mackie. Get up and hit him," said Dixon in a cloud of cigar smoke.

Mackie scrambled to his feet. He shook off the defeat with a dance of his feet and show of speed with the same combination he'd used a few minutes before.

"Stop dancing and come at me again," said Harvey.

"What do you mean, stop dancing?" said Mackie. "I'm keeping agile."

Mackie stepped forwards and offered the exact same combination of punches he'd just thrown. Harvey ducked down, slammed his fist into the boy's gut, then stood through his defence and took hold of his neck again. But this time, he used his momentum and lifted Mackie while kicking his legs away, then slammed him down onto the canvas and held him by his throat.

Mackie rolled away the second Harvey released him, then stood and let the flush of embarrassment drain from his face before beginning his bouncing again.

"Stop dancing and come at me," said Harvey, with his hands on his hips.

Mackie came to a stop. He strode up to Harvey, weaved in and out, from left to right, then issued a new series of punches, two body blows and the last aimed at Harvey's face. With relative ease, Harvey took hold of Mackie's arm and used the boy's momentum to force him into the rope, and once more, pinned him down with the heavy rope against his windpipe. It was only when he began to cough and

splutter that Harvey let him go and moved to the far side of the ring
to give him space to recover.

"You're not even fighting me," said Mackie. "What are you
doing?"

Harvey collected his jacket from the corner and pulled it on.

"Where do you think you're going?" said Dixon.

"Does the boy want a lesson or not?" said Harvey. "Does he want
to survive tonight? Because if he does, he needs to pay attention to
what I'm doing."

"And what is it you're doing?" said Mackie. "And of course I
want to survive."

"Listen, Mackie, you're a great boxer, or you will be one day."

"But?" said Dixon. "The boy has won every fight he's had."

"Boxing?" asked Harvey.

"Of course boxing," said Mackie. "Del, is this guy for real?"

Harvey listened to the boy's last words, then stepped over to him
and watched as he scurried away until he was cornered.

"You're a good boxer," said Harvey. "You're quick, you're accu-
rate and you follow through. Don't let them recover, whatever
happens. No matter how good the punch was, don't admire it.
Destroy the opposition."

"Cheers," said Mackie, unsure if Harvey's praise was genuine.

"But it's not enough," said Harvey.

"What's not enough?" said Dixon. He followed Harvey around
the edge of the ring and stared up from the concrete floor below.

"The fight is not an ordinary boxing match. It's not even an ordinary bare-knuckle fight. It's a fight to the death."

"Right?" said Dixon.

"So what are you saying?" asked Mackie.

Harvey removed his jacket once more and hung it on the ropes.
He rolled his neck from side to side, took a deep breath, and then
coaxed Mackie to his feet.

"No dancing," he said.

"Right," said Mackie, and he stood on the balls of his feet with his guard up.

"Good," said Harvey. "Now forget everything you know about boxing."

"Eh?" both Dixon and Mackie said together.

"Put your guard down."

Mackie lowered his guard with a nervous look at Dixon, who was lighting a new cigar and looking on with growing interest.

"I don't know who you're going to be up against tonight. If Del's right, John Cooper will have found a replacement. He'll be a boxer. He might be good. He might not. But that's not a chance you can afford, is it? So let's assume he's very good."

"I guess so," said Mackie. He began to rub his arms as the chill of the huge power station found his white, sweaty skin.

"But you'll have the advantage, won't you?" said Harvey.

"Will I?" said Mackie, with another glance at Dixon.

"Whoever it is that stands in front of you tonight, Mackie, will try to out-box you. He'll fight dirty if he has to. There's no rules in these matches. Am I right, Del?"

Dixon nodded.

"But you're not going to box him. You're going to watch his every move, dodge, duck, weave, whatever it is you need to do to work out how he fights."

"And then what?" said Mackie.

"When I'm done with you, Mackie, you'll no longer be a boxer. Being a boxer isn't good enough for what you need to do. In fact, I don't know how you've survived this long. I can only assume you've been up against like-minded mediocre boxers. But, like I said, being a boxer isn't good enough."

"So what do I need to be?" asked Mackie with apprehension in his voice.

Harvey closed the gap between the two men, stared the boy in the eye, and then shot his hand up once more to his throat.

"What you need to be, Mackie, is a killer."

CHAPTER THIRTY-FIVE

The car ride from the old slaughterhouse to the Golden Ring was short, but Tyler felt every bump in the road and swayed giddily with every turn they took. Nausea hung at the back of his throat with a wave of hot acid behind it. A layer of cold sweat formed on his brow in contrast to the hot, damp patches beneath his arms and the burning heat in the centre of his chest.

He stared at his open hands on his lap as if they weren't his own anymore. They were now like two good friends that had betrayed him. In the background, John Cooper spoke, slow and rough. Blurred slices of Jerry's rapid Irish filled the gaps.

Before his previous fights, his trainers had kept him focused, relaxed him with massages, and drowned him in sickening positive energy. John and Jerry's conversation was clouded in a deafening hum, and all Tyler could hear was Harvey's voice.

'*Control it.*'

He'd spoken the words matter-of-factly. It wasn't some hippy state of play on the mind. It was real.

'*Use it.*'

Although his sweaty hands were empty, they pulsed with electric tension. The fingertips twitched as unspent adrenaline sought a place to break free. The crunching of gristle and breaking bones from Jack's neck played on repeat. It was a feeling Tyler would never forget. How the man's head had reached its limit. How the muscles had stretched in Tyler's hands until the only resistance had been the spinal column, which snapped after the third brutal wrench.

Even Tyler's legs, which had wrapped around Jack's torso, still felt the twitching of his body. Even when the struggle had stopped and Jack's head had fallen forwards, twisted unnaturally, and his hands had ceased scrambling and fallen to the canvas, the body still twitched. Much like the adrenaline in Tyler's hands, the electricity within Jack's broken body sought an exit.

The stench of urine had come last. Tyler had heard about the muscles of a dead body relaxing. He'd seen it in documentaries and movies where a hard-nosed detective covers his face and offers a reticent quip. But all Tyler had felt as Jack's racing heart had reached the peak of its climbing crescendo and stopped as suddenly as if a switch had been flicked was pity.

He'd wanted to hug the man. He'd wanted to say he was sorry and take it all back. But John Cooper stared up at him through the ropes with glory in his eyes and had spoken those words.

"That's it, Tyler," said John. He slammed his hands onto the canvas in elation and laughed like a madman. "You're a killer. Did you hear me? You're a bleeding killer, Tyler."

"Tyler? Tyler. Did you hear me?"

The words were loud. Memories of how he'd cradled Jack's body were sucked into nothingness and John's sour breath roused Tyler from his daze as he leaned across the seat.

"Get out of the bleeding car, son. We're here."

Tyler peered through the car's side window as the front doors opened and filled the rear with a blast of cold air that found Tyler's damp sweat patches.

"The Golden Ring?" he asked.

"Where else?" said John, as Jerry pulled the rear door open for

Tyler to get out. "As soon as we get inside, get yourself downstairs and into the changing room. Don't talk to anyone. They'll mess with your head, especially if they're betting against you. Jerry, see to it he gets there. Mick, upstairs in my office."

"Right you are, John," said Jerry, and led the way into the pub with Tyler behind and John bringing up the rear. But just as his hand reached for the handle, Tyler spoke out.

"Wait," he said.

Jerry stopped.

"Tyler, this is no time to cock about, son. Remember what I told you would happen if you pulled out of the fight?"

"I'm not pulling out," replied Tyler. "But I want to see her. I want to see my mum before the fight. Just in case-"

"Just in case what?" spat John. "In case you don't make it? Don't be soft, Tyler."

John spoke the words with a warning tone and allowed a shadow of a doubt to wash across his face.

"I'll fight," said Tyler. He backed away from them both, and filled his chest with a deep long breath. "But only if I see my mum first. I need to see her. I need to say goodbye."

CHAPTER THIRTY-SIX

"Close the door, Mick," said John, as he dropped into his leather office chair and pulled himself close to the desk. "I've done a bit of thinking."

"Do you want a drink, John?" asked Mick, standing beside the crystal decanter, poised and ready to pour.

"No, Mick. Not tonight, mate. And you shouldn't either. We need to be on top form tonight. If it all kicks off downstairs, I don't want anyone's judgement clouded by booze, which leads me nicely into my idea."

"Are you getting everyone drunk, John?" said Nobby. "So they can't fight?"

"No, Nobby, but you're close. Keep your eyes and ears to the ground. If it sounds like all fingers point at us, I need to know. As soon as the fight is over, I'll send the girls around with trays of champagne. Whatever you do, don't bleeding drink it."

"You're not planning-" said Mick.

"Yes, I am, Mick. Remember, these men will be out for blood, potentially my blood, your blood and anyone's blood they can get their hands on. If it all goes south, it won't be until after the money has changed hands. By that time, the basement will be full of London's most dangerous criminals, all having a nap, leaving us enough time to make a getaway."

"You're going to run?" asked Mick. "After everything we've built here?"

"Everything we've built here won't be worth a lot if those slimy bastards downstairs have us in their cross-hairs, Mick. You'll be a wanted man. So will you, Nobby. You won't be able to walk to the shop to buy a paper and a pint of milk without looking over your shoulder. And it'll happen one day, when you least expect it. When we think we got away with it, we'll be taken down, cut into pieces, and slung in the river. When you was a kid, did either of you ever have races with your friends where you both throw a stick in the river and see which one reaches the bridge first?"

"Yeah," said Mick, nodding.

"Well, they'll be doing that with your legs and the legs of your wife. Do you get the picture?" said John.

Both Mick and Nobby nodded.

"Right. Good," said John, regaining his stride and opening his desk drawer. "I've made the arrangements. There's two tickets each for the Eurostar first thing in the morning."

"Are you sure about this, John?" asked Mick. "This is serious stuff. We can't go drugging the entire criminal community."

"So what's your plan then, brains?" said John. "You've had just as much time to think about all of this as I have. What plan did you come up with?"

"Well-"

"Well nothing," said John. "Believe me, I'd hate to leave this place behind and everything we've worked for, but if push comes to shove, we can start again. Maybe somewhere sunny?"

Nobby glanced up at Mick who turned away.

"Are you both clear on the plan?" asked John. "Keep your ears to the ground. I want to know if we're under suspicion. If we are, I'll signal the girls to do their thing, and we'll make our exit before the ceremonial exchange of money and while everyone is filling their gullets with champagne."

"What about the boy?" asked Mick.

"The boy? He'll be okay. A lesson learned and all that, Mick. Where is he anyway?"

"He's with his mum," said Nobby.

"Well get him out," said John. "He's been in there long enough. I want a word with him before the fight."

CHAPTER THIRTY-SEVEN

The car park of the Golden Ring was brimming with expensive luxury cars when Dixon's driver entered with the Mercedes. He was a quiet man who reminded Harvey of the man that used to drive his foster father around. Quiet, observant and in control. Harvey didn't ask his name. He just sat in the passenger seat preparing himself while Dixon reeled off endless spurts of spiteful monologue, mostly about the look on John Cooper's face when Mackie won, and how good it would feel to take the money off him.

"The first thing I'll do when Cooper hands me the keys to the ring is buy everyone a drink," said Dixon. "He's only had a few days to find a replacement. Mackie has been with me for over a year. Never lost a fight, have you, son?"

Harvey heard the slap of Dixon's hand on Mackie's leg, but Mackie was quiet. The words of wisdom Harvey had passed on were most likely running through his mind. The confident look on the boy's face had dropped to an expression of fear and self-loathing.

The driver turned and parked in a prime spot close to the building and facing the exit. The engine died. But before any doors opened, they waited for the van to park behind them. It was full of Dixon's men, all armed to the teeth and prepped for action.

"Right, boys," said Dixon. "Remember, nothing is going to happen until after the fight. So I've got until then to make some friends. Harvey, you concentrate on Mackie. Keep his chin up and keep him focused. If you hear anything, warn me. When the fight is over, and John Cooper has given me a bag full of money and the keys to his pub, that's when one of us will be slotted. Until then, it's a normal night at a prize fight, and we've got the winning boy. Is that clear?"

"Crystal," said the driver.

Harvey didn't reply. He pushed open his door, straightened his jacket and searched the parked cars for signs of life. Through the windscreen of a van parked fifty metres away, a few orange glows of cigarettes could be seen. But it wasn't a sign of someone about to jump them. With some of the most powerful men in London attending the fight, Harvey imagined there would be several armies nearby waiting for it all to kick off.

Dixon opened his door and climbed out, giving Harvey a distasteful look, as if he should have opened the door for him, as if he was some sort of king.

"Keep your men in the van," said Harvey, "and stay behind me."

"What, are you my minder now?" asked Dixon. "You just look after Mackie. I'll take care of myself. I didn't get this far having my hand held."

Harvey didn't reply. He led the way into the rear doors of the pub, which took him into the public bar. A band was warming up and a few of the locals glanced his way. But they turned away when Dixon followed him in. He walked straight through the bar hatch, and through another door that led down to the cellar.

The busy hum of multiple hushed conversations filled the space, which Harvey guessed to span further than the floor plan of the pub itself, with eight large columns that supported the building and framed a boxing ring in the centre of the room. The smell of old beer and cigar smoke tainted the air, and fluorescent lights created areas of intense brightness ringed by shadows. Harvey took a guess at the crowd being one hundred strong. Instead of the ring being surrounded by lines of chairs for the audience, a series of high tables had been provided, allowing five to six men at each table to enjoy an unobstructed view of the fight, and a place in the shadows to stand.

On each of the four sides of the ring, two tables were fortuned prime position. The tables were all taken except one, which Dixon claimed. He set his cigar down in the ashtray, slid his coat from his shoulders, allowing a girl in hot pants and a tiny top to take it from him, and then took a glass of champagne from the tray her colleague offered.

The girl turned to Harvey, smiled at him, and moved close enough for him to smell her thick perfume and say no to the drinks she offered.

Dixon leaned forwards to speak in Harvey's ear.

"Cooper isn't here yet. He'll make a grand entrance. Why don't you take Mackie out back and get him ready? I don't want him getting nervous," said Dixon. "The fight won't start for an hour, but warm him up, keep him hydrated and five minutes before you come back out, give him this."

Dixon slipped a little polythene bag of white powder into Harvey's inside pocket and tapped it twice. Then he turned to talk to the table behind them. Four unsmiling men with shaved heads, long Kashmir jackets and open collars stood with their hands in their pockets, eying Harvey with narrowed, suspicious eyes.

"Boys," said Dixon, in mock surprise as he turned away. Then he glanced back at Harvey. "I don't have to repeat myself, do I?"

Harvey gestured for Mackie to follow him through a set of doors. The hum of the room faded to a dull murmur, and flickering light lit a small corridor with one room on each side. Two dressing rooms.

A letter-sized piece of paper with the name Dixon in bold, black letters was pinned to one of the doors. Harvey walked inside. The room was small but clean with a slatted wooden bench, a single locker and walls that were thick with years of grey paint. A small shower cubicle and a toilet were at the end of the room with a tiled floor that reached out to the corridor.

Harvey dropped the cocaine into the toilet, flushed it and eyed Mackie, who looked nervous but was getting through it.

"Do you need help?" asked Harvey.

Mackie shook his head. "No."

"Good. I'll be back in a while," said Harvey. "Warm up while I'm gone."

"What do you mean warm up?" said Mackie, looking around the dingy changing room.

"I don't know. Do a dance or something," said Harvey.

He left Mackie to his own devices and stepped back into the corridor with the flickering light. Through a small window in the doors, Harvey could see the four men all listening to one of Dixon's anecdotes with a less-than-impressed look mirrored across all four of their faces.

Harvey pushed through the doors and headed straight to the stairs. At the top was the entrance to the bar where another staircase led up to the first floor. With a quick look both ways, he took the next staircase and reached a landing with four doors leading off it. The door to the front of the building was closed. From inside, Harvey recognised the deep, authoritative voice of John Cooper. There was the occasional pause as somebody else spoke, but it was too quiet for Harvey to hear.

Keeping close to the walls, Harvey edged away from Cooper's office and along the hallway. The next door was ajar with an oak floor, large leather couch and a big flat-screen TV on show through the small gap. Harvey moved past, but as he did, two men climbed the staircase behind him. Their voices grew louder in the stairwell and their heavy boots thundered on the old, wooden stairs.

Harvey froze then slipped into the room.

He watched as the three men appeared. One of them had been in the pub the night Harvey had met Tyler. The others were unknown but one had a thick Irish accent, was smaller and had the rough edges of a pikey. The old upstairs hallway echoed with their voices but another noise cut through the dull monotones of the men.

The stifled mumble of tears was coming from the door at the end of the hallway.

CHAPTER THIRTY-EIGHT

Something clawed at Tyler's insides as he pulled the door closed. He held his mum's sorrowful gaze until the last moment, and then let his fingers slip from the door handle. Closing off the sound of her tears inside, he placed the flat of his hand against the wood, as if somehow she would know, and would realise how sorry he was that all of this happened.

He felt, rather than heard, John Cooper behind him at the doorway to his office, so choosing to leave his mum on his own terms, Tyler let his hand fall away, then turned and joined John.

In the office, he chose a seat to the side of the desk, a wide armchair with artificial leather upholstery. It was a cheap choice in comparison to the luxurious recliner John had selected for his own comfort. It was symbolic, thought Tyler, of the man's greed and selfish style.

A true narcissist.

But as with many narcissists, John opened with artificial under-standing and comfort, much like the chair Tyler had chosen to sit on.

"I need you to focus now, Tyler," said John. "Now is not the time to fill your head with thoughts of your mother."

Tyler nodded. He couldn't meet the man eye to eye. Instead, he stared at the intricate patterns in the oak floor.

"In less than thirty minutes, you'll be toe to toe with Dixon's boy." John paused while Tyler began to think about the fight. "Are you ready?"

Again, Tyler nodded.

"Usually when you fight, you have a goal in mind. A belt or a trophy. Right?" asked John.

"Trophies," replied Tyler, still staring at the floor with his elbows resting on his knees.

"Look at me, son. I'm not talking to the top of your head," said John. The warm, faux comfort was lost and the words came out sharp and cold.

Tyler looked up at him.

"Do you want some advice, son?" said John, retaining his harsh tones. "Forget about your mum. For the next hour or so, at least. Just forget about her. She's not going anywhere. We've given her painkillers. She's in good hands, Tyler. Focus on the fight. Focus on getting Dixon's boy down."

"Have you seen him?" asked Tyler, his voice still thick with emotion.

"Mackie?" asked John. "Of course I have."

"Did he beat your last fighter?"

With a slow nod of his head, John confirmed.

"He died then?" asked Tyler. "Your fighter? He died."

"Yes, Tyler. He died. It was..." He sought the words, but Tyler knew whatever word he chose would sound callous from the man's bitter mouth. "Unfortunate."

"How long did he last?"

"How many rounds? Or how many fights?"

"Both."

"One and one," said John. "I was told he was a dead cert."

"What was his name?"

"Oh, Tyler. What does it matter?"

"What was his name, John?" Tyler's voice rose and shut down John's attempt to make the dead boy insignificant.

"Fraser," said John. "His name was Fraser. That's all we knew. He was a street kid. Nothing to lose. You know the sort?"

"And how much do you stand to win if I beat Dixon's boy?"

"That's not something you need to trouble yourself with, is it, Tyler?" said John. "In fact, that's getting awfully close to the line that you, sunshine, do not cross."

"What about me?" asked Tyler. "You said we wouldn't have to worry about money. You told me I'd be able to afford proper care for my mum. How much will we get? My mum and me?"

"If I was you, Tyler, I'd be more concerned with what happens to her if you lose."

"That's not going to happen, John," said Tyler, standing and shunting the chair back. "When I go into that ring tonight, I'm not going in there for you. I'm going in there for Fraser. I'm going in there for myself. And I'm going in there for my mum. I'll be taking my winnings and you won't see me again."

"You're not in the best place to make demands."

Quick as a flash, Tyler reached across the desk, grabbed John by his collar and hauled him out of his chair, dragging him across the leather insert and knocking the phone and pens to the floor. He slammed John into the wall with one hand on his throat and the other poised to deliver a deadly punch.

"Now you listen to me, John Cooper," said Tyler. "I got myself into this. I'll get myself out of it. A deal is a deal."

"You just overstepped the mark, Tyler," said John, trying to regain the upper hand.

"Look around you, John. Your bodyguards aren't here and don't even think about reaching for your pocket."

For just a fraction of a moment, John's eyes betrayed his fear, then returned to their cool, controlling glare.

"One hundred thousand pounds," said John. "I'll give you one hundred thousand pounds to go down there and kill Mackie with your bare hands."

Tyler let the number hang in the air for a moment then lowered his voice.

"Two," he said. "I want two hundred thousand pounds. One for me, and one for my mum."

"Oh, come on-" John began, but Tyler strengthened his grip.

"Two hundred thousand pounds, and if you try anything, I'll tear you apart limb from limb."

"Okay, okay," said John. "Two hundred grand. I can do that."

The two locked eyes for a moment then Tyler relaxed his hand.

"So now we've come to an agreement, Tyler-"

"And what about my mum?" said Tyler. "If I lose, she needs care."

But John Cooper emitted a cruel and hate-filled laugh.

"After that little demonstration of your emotional instability, Tyler?"

He straightened his jacket and smoothed out the non-existent creases with the palms of his hands. He snatched a handgun from inside his jacket and pointed it at Tyler. He stepped closer, then placed the gun beneath Tyler's chin, pushing up and back until Tyler's head hit the wall behind him.

"I'll tell you what I'll do. If you win, you'll get your two hundred grand. But how about this for motivation? If you lose, I'll take this gun, and I'll stick it in your dear old mum's mouth. But before I pull the trigger, I'll tell her how much of a coward her son was. And I'll tell her exactly how Mackie crushed your skull. I'll be sure to include the gory details, Tyler. And only then, once I've seen her fall apart at the seams at the loss of her beloved son, will I pull the trigger and end her misery and pain. So stop cocking about, get downstairs, get in that ring, and win that bleeding fight."

CHAPTER THIRTY-NINE

"I'm not going to hurt you," said Harvey with his finger to his lips.

He checked to make sure the landing was clear and John Copper's goons weren't loitering then pushed the door, not closing it fully, as the handle had been removed from the inside. The woman was silent, but her eyes were wide and fearful, watching Harvey's every move. A foul stench came from the corner of the room where a bucket had been placed. The curtains were closed but were thin, allowing a fog of streetlight to pass through, ghostlike, and touch the edges of the items in the room like a mother might smooth a child's hair.

"Are you Mrs Thomson?" he asked, his voice reduced to a whisper.

Mrs Thomson's eyes shone in the poor light like glistening diamonds on the carcass of the dead. She waved him over with two feeble flicks of her wrist, then patted the mattress for him to sit beside her. The fear had gone from her eyes, replaced by an inquisitive, curious stare.

Harvey took a step forwards, checking through the tiny gap in the door again.

"Sit with me," she said, her hoarse voice no louder than a whisper. "Where I can see you."

There was a confidence in the woman's voice; she was unafraid. He sat on the side of the bed with his back to the window. Her hand reached up from where she lay, felt his face and turned it to the light, left then right.

Harvey remained silent.

It was coming.

She licked her lips in a futile attempt to ease her speech. There was no water for her and Harvey could have crept out to find some, but something held him still.

"I know you," she said.

Three words.

"Like the angels above know the devil below, I know you."

She let her hand fall and lay it across her stomach. She turned away and stared back at the ceiling.

Harvey didn't reply.

"You're the foster boy who lost his sister. He spoke of you. It was like you were his boy. So proud, he was." It was clear she was recalling memories from a time long ago. Even in the dim light, with her prominent features, Harvey could see she would have been a beautiful woman in her day. "I know what he used to do, the type of man he was." She paused as if wondering if she should carry on, then sighed and gave in. "I know what you do. I know what he trained you to do."

"I'm not here to hurt you," said Harvey.

"Well, you should be," she replied. Her whisper was cold and sharp. "Take me away from all this. Put an end to it all."

Harvey didn't reply.

"He could have. He would have too if he saw me like this."

"You're wrong," said Harvey. "He was a good man. He'd never-"

"You didn't know him like I did," she said. "My Julios."

Hearing somebody speak with so much affection for Julios

warmed Harvey. He'd never heard it before and he wanted her to carry on. But it wasn't the time.

"Mrs Thomson, I need to tell you something," said Harvey.

"Don't waste your breath. I'm dying," she replied. "If you're not here to help me, then go. You may as well leave."

Her hand slid across the old mattress and found Harvey's. Though her hands shook and her body clenched from visible stabs of pain, the strength of her grip surprised Harvey. Wide, moist eyes followed his as her cold, trembling hand led his to her chest.

"Do you feel that, Harvey Stone?" she asked.

It was the first time she'd spoken his name. A confirmation of the things she knew.

Harvey shook his head.

"No," he whispered. "I feel nothing."

"That's because there's nothing to feel," she replied.

"I was there, you know?" said Harvey. He didn't know why; it just came out.

"I thought you might have been."

A burning behind Harvey's eyes and a swell in his chest took the words by the hand and together they ventured into the light.

"It was my fault. I saw it all," said Harvey. "But I couldn't stop it."

Mrs Thomson peered up at Harvey, but let him speak. There was no malice or anger in her eyes, just understanding.

"There's nothing I wouldn't do to bring him back," he finished.

She squeezed Harvey's hand.

"Take me to him, Harvey," she said. He felt her pull his hand upward, to which he offered no resistance. Even when she opened his fingers to encircle her throat, he dared not pull away. And when she closed his hand around her tiny, feeble neck, she smiled.

"I'm glad it was you," she whispered. "He would've wanted this."

She increased the pressure on his fingers, a signal that she was ready. Although her eyes glowed in the pale orange light, the tears that moistened them did not roll onto her face.

"Do it, Harvey," she whispered. "Take me to him. There's nothing for me here now."

Countless times, Harvey had squeezed the life from men. But never a woman. Never someone who had been so close, yet so far away. There were ways of easing the passing without the need for brutality. His fingers sought her windpipe through the loose flesh on her neck until the muscles around it fought to protect the airway.

He began to squeeze.

"Look after him, Harvey," she rasped, squeezing her eyes closed, and embracing the oncoming journey with what appeared to be delight. "Take care of my boy."

Harvey released her, drawing his hand away.

In a panic, she reached for his hand, easing it back to her throat.

"Don't stop," she whispered.

"I'm sorry," said Harvey, searching for the words that would make it right, but knowing deep inside that nothing could ever repair the damage he'd done. Despite only knowing the woman for a few minutes, for the second time in his life, he'd failed to save the ones she loved. "I couldn't stop it. He's gone."

Thoughts of her own death sank from the frail lady's face and motherly love coaxed energy from some hidden part of her.

"Where?" she said. Her wild eyes began to stream. "When?"

"Two nights ago," replied Harvey. He couldn't meet her eyes. "There was a fire."

"That can't be," she said. "You're lying."

"I wish I was. I let him down. I let you down. And I let Julios down again."

"No, it can't be," she said. "He was just here."

CHAPTER FORTY

"Ladies and gentlemen," began the master of ceremonies, as Harvey stepped into the basement and headed towards the changing rooms. "Welcome to the Golden Ring, the home of the back street, bare-knuckle boxing tournaments for as long as I can remember. And tonight, have we got a treat for you. But before we introduce our two very brave boys, I'd like to say a few words."

The voice of the MC faded away to the hum of the air-conditioning as Harvey stepped into the narrow hallway with a flickering light. To his right, Harvey now realised, Tyler would be preparing himself, psyching himself up for the fight.

He stopped at the doorway. Behind him were all of London's hardest men in one room. Every single one of them would have a wager on and every single one of them was there to see a fight to the death.

Harvey stepped back. He glanced through the small window in the door. Escaping unseen would be impossible. There were van loads of armed men in the car park. Even if he did take Tyler and run for it, they wouldn't get far. Whatever happened, nothing could wipe the shame Harvey felt. Guilt and sorrow hung like weights from some place inside of him, some place he'd never been able to reach. Like an itch, it tormented him and meeting Tyler had awoken it.

Whatever happened, the boy needed to survive. It was the last thing he could do for Julios.

"And without further ado," said the MC, "let's meet our first fighter. Ladies and Gentlemen, let me introduce you to Tyler Tornado Thomson."

Before Tyler emerged from his changing room and while the criminal audience erupted in eager applause behind him, Harvey lifted a fire extinguisher from its hook on the wall and stepped into Mackie's room.

The boy was sitting on the slatted wooden bench, his head resting in his hands. He looked up just as Harvey slammed the fire extinguisher into his face. The force of the blow sent the boy reeling backwards over the bench. But he stood and launched the bench at Harvey, following it up by running at him and slamming his shoulder into Harvey's gut, forcing him against the hard, painted brick wall.

Pinned to the wall, Harvey used his elbows to knock the boy backward, but in the limited time he'd had with him earlier that day, Mackie had listened to everything he'd said. With an animal-like strength, he tossed Harvey across the room into the wash basin. It ripped from the wall and tore the water pipe.

Freezing water gushed into the air and rained down on them both. But the reprise gave Harvey enough time to pull off his wet jacket. He rolled his neck from side to side and coaxed Mackie toward him.

The boy had listened to what Harvey had told him. He stood there waiting for Harvey to attack with water dripping from his brow.

"I thought you were on my side?" said Mackie.

"You can't fight him," said Harvey. "I can't let you go out there. I don't want to hurt you any more than I have to, but one way or another, you aren't fighting tonight."

"Why not?" replied Mackie. "That's why I'm here. I'm going to tear his head off." His teeth were bared and his wide eyes showed black holes for pupils.

"I can't let you do that," said Harvey with a sigh. He rolled his neck, felt the familiar bite of his inner beast, and then stepped forward.

There was no combination of rehearsed punches offered to Harvey, and Mackie didn't bounce from one foot to the other. He stood ready, watching Harvey's every move. In just a few short hours, Harvey had taught the boy how to kill, not fight. The difference was what had separated Harvey from nearly every man he'd been up against in his life. Fighting is one thing; you train to hurt people. Killing is another; usually, the first move is the last if done right.

Mackie had shown promise. His strength and speed combined with Harvey's knowledge had formed a lethal young boy.

"It needs to be me," said Harvey, and he launched an attack while the boy contemplated the words. Harvey gave an open-handed stab at his windpipe. But Mackie was quick. His reactions were lightning fast and he knocked Harvey's hand away with ease, sidestepped, and delivered a sharp blow to Harvey's kidney.

Deep breaths eased the shock and Harvey stepped away.

"I thought I told you to follow up, not to wait?" said Harvey.

"I thought I'd give you a chance," replied Mackie.

Harvey straightened, dropped his arms to his sides and picked up his jacket.

"Where are you going?" asked Mackie, stepping over to block Harvey's exit.

Harvey swung his jacket round in a wide arc. He caught the sleeve as the confused-looking Mackie turned to see what was happening.

But it was too late for him.

Harvey pulled the thick leather tight against Mackie's neck, twisting it to tighten the grip and close off the boy's airway. A sharp kick to the back of his legs dropped Mackie to his knees and both hands gripped the jacket, trying in vain to pull it from his throat.

Harvey slammed his knee into the back of his lungs, forcing the last remaining breath from Mackie's body. Then, keeping his knee in place, he forced Mackie's head back with the taught leather jacket fastened around his neck.

"That's the last lesson you'll ever learn, Mackie," said Harvey, as he strengthened his grip. "Never give anyone a chance."

He squeezed harder and watched as the boy's face morphed through shades of red, from pink flesh tones to the deep, cherry colour of blood. Tiny spatters of saliva flew from Mackie's lips with the last breaths his body would take. The battle-hardened boy whimpered as he succumbed to death.

It was a sound Harvey had heard too often. The brave face of masculinity was typically a facade, underneath which, in most men, a child lives and breathes, and when the cold hand of death approaches, the child cries out.

It wasn't until Mackie's lifeless hands released their grip on Harvey's jacket and his body slumped to the cold, concrete floor that Harvey released the pressure. Water continued to rain down on Harvey, breaking the silence as the amplified and muffled voice of the MC came through the thick walls.

"And now, on behalf of the one and only, Mr Dixon, our guest fighter tonight and current champion, let's hear it for Mackie." The audience applauded once more as Mackie lay motionless at Harvey's feet in a pool of cold and bloodied water.

Harvey hung his jacket on a hook fixed to the wall. He pulled off his soaking white t-shirt and hung it beside the jacket, then took three deep, long breaths before stepping out beneath the flickering light and through the double doors to where a sea of confused faces greeted him with wide eyes.

But above the heads of the confused, criminal faces, standing alone in the centre of the ring, one face stared at Harvey.

Harvey met Tyler's gaze. They locked onto each other as the

murmurs around them rose to a deafening hum of curses and taunts. But nothing could break Harvey's focus. No crude curse or threatening taunt found its way to Harvey's mind.

It was payback time for Julios and his son was ready to receive the payment.

CHAPTER FORTY-ONE

A murmur among the men below and all around Tyler grew into a hum of confused questions as each of the guests looked from Harvey to Del Dixon and back to Tyler, whose heart sank in the pit of his stomach. He backed into his corner to watch Harvey Stone pull himself to the edge of the ring and step through the ropes.

With outrage written all over his face, Del Dixon shook his head at Harvey, who ignored the gesture and began to roll his neck from side to side. He didn't offer a menacing look or a threatening stare. Instead, Harvey simply nodded once at Tyler and prepared for the fight.

The hum of the crowd had worked itself to an excited buzz. New bets were being placed, cigars were lit and trays of champagne seemed to float across the tops of the grey, bald and shaved heads as if they were at the whim of a river that ran around the ring.

The ref took to the centre of the ring, held his hands in the air to silence the buzzing crowds, and cleared his throat.

He waved for both Harvey and Tyler to join him.

The fascinated crowd listened on with awe.

The ref looked between Harvey and Tyler as if he were delivering bad news.

"Tonight, one of you will die," said the ref. His choice of words was designed more for the crowd's amusement than as a warning to the fighters. "There's no gloves and no rules except one. The last man standing wins."

The crowd erupted into a frenzy of cheers and taunts aimed mainly at Harvey, the smaller of the two men.

"Lights please," called the ref.

The lights dimmed all around, leaving the ring lit by two huge spotlights in the ceiling. The hum of the audience fell to a whisper and the ref ordered them both back to their corners.

Finding John at the most prominent table, Tyler searched for answers, but received only an unsmiling nod of the head. John ran his finger across his throat then pointed to the ceiling.

"Are you ready?" asked the ref, as if Tyler's distraction was holding up the fight.

He nodded.

The ref caught his eye one last time then glanced at Harvey. He brought his arm up then swung it down, issuing the command to fight. Then he stepped out of the way and climbed through the ropes. As the ref in a fight with no rules, his job was over.

Harvey stepped forwards and gestured for Tyler to come at him. But Tyler froze. It was his father's only friend. He couldn't fight him.

The murmur of the crowd grew in volume like a slowly approaching wave. But when Harvey landed the first punch, a jab to Tyler's gut, the wave crashed and the crowd erupted.

In their eyes, the fight had begun. But in Tyler's, he saw only one way out.

"Fight me," said Harvey over his guard as he ducked and weaved and planted a series of jabs into Tyler's ribs. "Don't just stand there. Fight me."

Harvey landed one more across Tyler's jaw. It was a sweet punch that rocked Tyler from his daze. Something stirred inside him. A growl of distaste and the warmth of emotions.

"That's it," said Harvey as Tyler pushed himself out of the corner. "Control it."

As if to make sure the beast was indeed waking, Harvey jabbed twice then landed a hook that grazed Tyler's ear and enabled Tyler to grab hold of Harvey and bring him close.

"What's going on?" he asked, "I thought-"

But Harvey delivered an uppercut to Tyler's gut in the same spot as before. The punch caught Tyler off-guard and left him winded, so he moved away, and began to bounce from foot to foot.

"Get on with it," shouted a bald man from the crowd. His thick London accent made the sentence sound as if it were all one word.

Raising his guard, Tyler moved in with a combination of his own. The final of the four punches caught Harvey square in the face and sent him back to the corner, where Tyler followed him and rained in blow after blow to Harvey's stomach. Feigning fatigue, he leaned in close to Harvey.

"Fight me, Tyler," said Harvey, and he shoved him away.

Before Tyler could recover, Harvey was back on him. A beer bottle skidded across the canvas as Harvey rained punches in from every angle, the last of which caught Tyler's nose, causing the growl in the pit of his stomach to claw up to his chest.

"For your dad," said Harvey, as he came in for another attack.

But the beast saw it coming. Tyler dodged to one side and coiled like a spring then landed a blow to Harvey's face with the full weight of his body behind it, which sent Harvey to the floor.

"That's more like it," shouted one man who hung onto the ropes like he was a caged animal. "Get in there, son."

But Tyler watched with his arms by his sides as Harvey stood and came back at him with a series of punches.

"Hit me," shouted Harvey, and punched Tyler. "I said fucking hit me." He punched Tyler again then waited for a reaction.

But none came.

"Come on, Tyler," said Harvey, as he punched Tyler square in the gut. "Hit me."

'Control it.'

"Hit me," shouted Harvey.

'Use it.'

With his face up close to Tyler's, Harvey leaned into him, resting his fatigued arms on the boy's shoulders.

"Kill me," he whispered, then moved away to catch Tyler's eye. He nodded. "Kill me for your dad. It's all I have to give."

Tyler stared down at the man he'd met only a few days earlier but what seemed like a lifetime ago. The last connection to his father was standing in front of him, coiling for a punch and then releasing.

The blow rocked Tyler back to his heels.

"Hit him, Tyler," screamed John from the side of the ring. "Don't just bleeding stand there."

But Tyler couldn't move.

"I said kill me, Tyler," Harvey screamed in his face, and shoved him backwards. "Kill me, Tyler." Harvey stood in front of him, opening up his guard, and planted his feet flat on the canvas floor. "Come on. Hit me. Just do it. Kill me, Tyler. Please."

"Tyler, you've got three seconds before I go upstairs and open your mum up, sunshine. I'll cut her bleeding heart out and bring it down here for you to see," said John.

The beast climbed into Tyler's mind.

"Kill me," said Harvey, his anguished face pleading with Tyler as he shoved him across the ring.

"Three," called John. "I'll cut her from top to bottom, sunshine."

The beast took a deep breath.

"Come on. For your dad, Tyler. I'm open," said Harvey.

"Two. Tyler, this is your last chance," said John, and from the corner of his eye, Tyler caught the glint of a blade being pulled from John's jacket.

The beast rolled its neck from side to side. Tyler's huge frame coiled like a snake with his massive fist clenched tight.

Harvey dropped to his knees and held his arms out wide, inviting Tyler to attack him.

"Just do it. Just finish me, Tyler," screamed Harvey.

"One."

CHAPTER FORTY-TWO

The sound of the automatic gunfire that shredded the ceiling and rained broken glass down on the crowd cut through the tension like a hot knife through butter. The excited audience of hardened men and trophy wives dropped to the floor with a crash of broken champagne flutes and sought refuge behind anything solid. Tables were dragged to the floor and the sea of heads that had gazed up at Harvey became a tangled mass of arms and legs, as men covered their wives from danger.

The gunfire stopped.

Harvey, who was kneeling in the centre of the ring with Tyler lying flat on the floor beside him, looked out at the door to the staircase. Five men, black as the night, took confident steps across broken glass into the room. They strode in formation with the largest and ugliest at the front and his men behind him in a V-shape.

He let loose another short burst of gunfire and the last of the lights blew out.

Harvey didn't move an inch.

One of the men with a shaved head who had spoken to Dixon

earlier raised a handgun above the toppled table he was hiding behind. He fired off three rounds, all of which found the rear wall.

One of the intruders stepped out of formation, strode across the floor and opened up on the mass of people hiding behind the tables. The gunfire fell silent again, leaving the grunts of dying men and the whimpers of injured and dying women to fill the space.

"Any more brave men in here?" said the lead man.

The room fell silent.

"I didn't think so," he said. His voice was deep like a bass, and his accent was London through and through. "How about you?" He kicked out at a fat, bald man who lay across his wife on the floor in a protective pose, which gave way as he scrambled away from her and the man's boots. "No brave men in here then?" said the man, as he raised the automatic weapon and tucked his elbow into his side to take the weight.

"How about you, fella?" he said, as his eyes landed on Harvey. "Feeling brave tonight?"

"You've got no idea, mate," replied Harvey.

"Is that supposed to be funny?" said the man, as his four men joined him by the side of the ring. "What are you, some kind of tough guy?"

Harvey didn't reply.

The man looked down at Tyler on the canvas and then back at Harvey.

"Who's winning?" he asked.

"You're the one with the gun," said Harvey. "I'd say you're winning for the time being."

The intruder gazed up at Harvey and cocked his head with what appeared to be fascination.

"I'm looking for Del Dixon," he said at last. "Where can I find him?"

Harvey didn't reply.

"For a man with a smart mouth, you don't say much, do you?"

"Do I look like an information kiosk? Why don't you ask a few of the guests? I'm sure they'd be only too happy to oblige," replied Harvey.

Beyond the shoulders of the men, a single figure crawled towards the doorway.

The man talking to Harvey snapped around to his friends. His long thick dreadlocks trailed the movement of his head and swung around to his front.

"Find him," he ordered. "If anyone lies, shoot them."

The comment raised a few gasps and murmurs from the crowd on the floor all around the ring.

"Silence," the man shouted, and let a three-round burst pepper the ceiling. "Del Dixon, where are you?"

"He's by the-" called a woman, who was quickly silenced by her husband.

The man focused on the voice in the dark and trod across the broken glass to where he found her, wrestling her husband's hand from her mouth. "If they want Del, they can have him," she snapped at her husband. "Then they can get out of here and leave us alone."

The hot muzzle of the automatic grazed her rosy cheek. She winced and pulled away.

"Where?" said the man.

"By the door," the woman replied with regret in her voice. Harvey caught the shine of her husband's bald head as he shook it from side to side in dismay.

Beside the door, two of the intruders hauled Del Dixon to his feet and dragged him by his armpits through the tangle of limbs. They heaved him onto the canvas where he rolled to the centre away from their hands and stood beside Harvey, eying the men with caution as each one of them moved to guard one side of the ring.

There was no escape.

"If anyone tries to run anyway," the lead man announced, "there's an automatic rifle waiting to say hello at the top of those stairs. For the time being, this fight is over. All bets are off."

He climbed up onto the canvas and ducked beneath the rope, then circled Del Dixon as a lion might orbit its prey.

"You all might be wondering what my brothers and I are doing here. What is it we want? So I'll tell you."

He towered over Del Dixon, placed one big hand on the smaller man's shoulder, and looked out at the crowd.

"Up until two days ago, my brothers and I had one more brother, our youngest sibling. He chose not to work in the family business and we didn't see him often. But we loved him nonetheless." He nodded at one of his brothers who slid a small fuel can beneath the rope onto the canvas. "Two days ago, Del Dixon killed him in an attempt to win this fight."

Murmurs and whispers started to grow as the crowd began to see the outcome.

"Silence," the lead man said. "The next person to speak or move will be shot."

The room once more fell silent and the lead man turned to Harvey.

"You, grab that can."

Harvey got to his feet and collected the fuel can.

The lead man nodded at Del Dixon. There was no instruction necessary. Del Dixon's angry face turned to horror as the smell of the fuel hit him and reality set in. Harvey soaked Dixon's clothes and hair, and paid special attention to Dixon's feet, making sure his leather shoes were saturated. It was a trick he'd learned from Julios to ensure the victim couldn't run away.

"No," said Dixon. "Stop. It wasn't me."

"You look like you've done this before," said the lead man, ignoring Dixon. He held out a lighter in his steady hand and gazed at Harvey with wonder.

Harvey didn't reply. But for a second, the light from the stairwell caught movement. It was John Cooper.

Taking the lighter and crouching at Dixon's feet, Harvey looked up to enjoy the final expression of terror on Dixon's face.

"It wasn't me," said Dixon. "Don't do this. It wasn't me or my men."

"Any last requests?" said the man. "Is there anything you want the world to know?"

Dixon was breathing hard, the fumes accelerating his hyperventilation. He stared up at the intruder who loomed over him.

"I'm going to come back and bleeding haunt you."

"Not if my brother haunts you first," said the man, and nodded at Harvey.

Harvey sparked the lighter.

CHAPTER FORTY-THREE

The rush of flames igniting Dixon's agonised body sent the man into a blind frenzy. He bounced from the ropes as he tried to escape the ring and fell backwards, writhing and screaming.

But the scene was too much for the hardened crowd. As if it were coordinated, men emerged from the tables they hid behind, wielding handguns, and all hell broke loose. Harvey dove to the floor, covering Tyler as the lead man's body was peppered with shots from all angles until his knees buckled and he fell forwards onto Dixon.

Harvey rolled, pulling Tyler with him until they dropped from the ring and landed beside the still-twitching body of one of the brothers.

Automatic gunfire from the far side of the ring, along with many single handgun shots, sang out in the darkness. Only the burst of muzzle flash and the flames of Dixon's charred and squirming body lit the scene.

Flashes of muzzle fire near the stairwell blocked the exit. With one hand holding Tyler down, Harvey reached into the ring, grabbed the fuel can and began tearing a strip of clothing from the body of the dead yardie brother.

In near darkness, he knotted the strip of material, soaked it in fuel, and then stuffed it into the fuel can, wedging the knot tight into the hole.

"Get ready, Tyler," he said, as he lit the end of the rag, reached back and launched the can at the wall beside the stairwell. Flames burst from the wall as the plastic can split and burning fuel sprayed out in all directions.

"Now. Go."

He pulled Tyler to his feet and, for a brief moment, the gunfire stopped until they were halfway across the room. Then the automatic weapons opened up again. The wooden beams that supported the floor above took the flame, and like dry grass in a breeze, the fire rushed across the ceiling, burning blues and yellows.

Then the screams started.

Women made a beeline for the door as Harvey and Tyler reached the stairwell, but the intruders gunned down the criminal wives where they stood. With one foot on the first step, Harvey looked back to see two men with shaved heads attacking the last remaining brother. Both of them were cut down, and they skidded face first on the broken glass across the floor.

The flames now encircled the room. The dry, wooden, panelled walls crackled and popped as the heat intensified and the flames found fresh fuel. More than a dozen people remained alive, hiding behind furniture but too scared to run for the door.

The remaining brother looked up at Harvey. He cocked his head at Harvey's lack of fear, then nodded. A sign he was free to run. The man would die with his brothers.

Harvey shoved Tyler forwards and the two men ran up the stairs and found relative cool air on their scorched faces. The public bar was empty and the pair stopped at the top of the stairs, hearing the screaming of burning men and women below.

"I need to get my mum out," said Tyler, forcing the sounds of the dying from his mind.

Harvey nodded and glanced up the stairs.

"I'll wait for you out the back," he said. "I'll find us some wheels."

Tyler held his gaze, finding it difficult to break away, until Harvey turned to leave.

"Don't leave without us," said Tyler.

Stopping in the doorway, Harvey looked back and met his eyes.

"I won't," he said.

Tyler took the stairs two at a time. The door to his mum's room was locked, so he stepped back, his adrenaline still pumping, and slammed the heel of his foot into the wood. The door crashed open with the sound of splintering wood and Tyler crouched down beside his mum.

"Mum, it's me," he said. "We've got to go."

He nudged her shoulder to wake her.

"Mum, come on, it's me. You need to get up," he said, and nudged her harder. Her body rocked but still, she didn't move.

Using both hands, he gripped her shoulders and shook her.

"Mum, the place is on fire," he said, as the tears began to well up and his throat swelled. "Mum. Please."

He gripped her lifeless hand, resisting the urge to scream. Instead, he let his head fall onto her stomach.

"Please," he whispered, and brought her hand to his mouth to kiss the cold skin.

"Very touching," said a voice from behind him. The accent was familiar, but far removed from Tyler's mind. "I think you'll find you're a touch too late."

The beast growled inside Tyler's chest, long and guttural.

"John said you wanted to be with her. At least now I won't have to drag your fat carcass up the stairs."

A flash of light pulsed behind Tyler's eyes. He lifted his head and took a final look at his mother, wiping her loose hair from her brow and smoothing it behind her ears how she liked it.

"Up," said Jerry. "I haven't got all day. Some of us have trains to catch."

A twitch of nerves in Tyler's neck faded when he rolled his head from side to side, stretching the muscles.

He lay his mother's hands on her lap then bent forward to kiss her forehead.

The noise of a shotgun being armed cracked in the tiny room.

"Goodbye, mum," he said. But he found no more words to accompany them.

The twin barrels of the shotgun touched the back of his head, hard and steely cold, like the fingers of death himself.

With slow and deliberate movements, Tyler raised his arms and stood, then turned to find Jerry staring back at him with the cold, hard stare of a man who'd won.

The beast smiled.

CHAPTER FORTY-FOUR

The rear doors of the Golden Lion smashed open with the hard kick of Harvey's boot. The bite of the freezing wind found his naked torso, but the adrenaline that flowed through him blazed like the fires of hell. He was greeted by five men who all stepped from the side door of a van with shaved heads, tattoos and bomber jackets. Each of them brandished a selection of bats and knives.

"You've got to be kidding me," said Harvey.

"Nobody gets out alive," said the frontman.

A burst of automatic gunfire could be heard from the basement below then two single shots of a handgun silenced it. A lick of flames showed itself in the stairwell then retreated, leaving behind a mask of flickering oranges and yellows as the fire crept up the stairs in its unquenchable hunger for fresh fuel.

"I don't think there's much chance of that happening," replied Harvey.

But he was cut short as one of the men came at him with a wild swing of his bat. Harvey ducked as the bat missed his face by a few inches then reached up, grabbed the man's arm and twisted it until the wooden weapon fell from his grip and into Harvey's hand.

Keeping the grip on the man's arm, Harvey swung the bat in his left hand, familiarising himself with its weight. Then he gave the arm a final twist and pushed up until the crack of shattering bones induced agonised screams from the man. Harvey let him drop to his knees, then passed the bat to his right hand, swung it and delivered a blow to the man's head that spattered blood across his awestruck friends.

"Now we're equal," said Harvey, kicking the man's body to the ground. He rolled his head from side to side, felt the two satisfying clicks, and waited for the men to come at him, as they always did.

And they did.

Another man ran at him, carving a knife from side to side in long, sweeping arcs designed to break Harvey's guard. Taking one step back, Harvey shunted the blunt end of the bat into the man's face, stunning him long enough for Harvey to turn the blade in the man's hand and force it into his throat. Another forceful kick with the heel of his boot sent the second man onto the first. But there was no reprise.

All three remaining men came at Harvey, two with bats, one with a knife.

They closed in on three sides, attacking all at once. The first swing of a bat sent Harvey ducking low where he destroyed the kneecaps of the man to his right. But the knife lunged at him while he was low in a straight stab aimed for his gut. Harvey dropped onto his back, swung up with the bat and felt the man's wrist shatter under the blow. The last man with the bat took aim at Harvey's legs. There was no time to move or attack and the blow found his thigh with a hard, dull stab of pain.

The man with the broken wrist began to kick as Harvey rolled to his side, and once more, the bat found Harvey's back. A boot connected with Harvey's face, shattering his nose. The man with the broken wrist leaned over Harvey and peered into his eyes, looking for some kind of understanding.

"I told you, nobody gets out alive," he said, then spat in Harvey's face and waved the man with the bat closer. "Finish him off, Ted."

Ted stepped closer. He positioned himself beside Harvey's head then raised the bat high, coiled to deliver the hardest blow he could. Harvey braced for the hit. There was no room to move and not enough time to think. But as the man's back reached its zenith and his face contorted to summon all his strength, the sound of shattering glass from above tore his eyes from Harvey's head and the lifeless body of a man took him to the ground.

With barely a pause to think, Harvey swung at the last man's legs, rolled, then stood over him. He lifted his chin with the end of his bat then raised it for the final blow.

A screech of brakes and the crunch of tyres on gravel a few metres away stopped him. The side door slid open. Its metallic click was loud in the now-silent night, filled only with the distant sirens of the fire brigade and police. A familiar voice called out. The voice of reason.

"Harvey," cried Melody, "get in the van."

He stopped and met Melody's eyes. She was half in and half out of the van, reaching for him with a pleading gaze.

"You don't need to do this," she said. Her eyes darted to the building behind him. Tiny orange sparks found the cool night air and wafted past Harvey's face. Then, like a pack of hungry wolves, the flames reached out of the doors, searching for food to devour. "Come on."

Harvey stared back at the man on the ground, who waited for him to make his decision with wide, hopeful eyes.

With a glance back into the fire and then to Melody, Harvey tossed the bat across the car park. There was something missing. A feeling. He no longer felt the warm, guttural growl of his inner beast. The desire to punish the man was further from his mind. He saw with clarity a human being lying on the ground beneath him, beaten and broken.

Harvey stepped away. He could hear Melody and Reg calling to him from Reg's van. But their voices were no match for his thoughts as they sought to ease the beast inside him. He clung to the side of the van, felt Melody's hands clawing for him to climb inside, and heard the growing wails of the approaching emergency services.

He tore himself away from Melody, but locked eyes with her in the firelight.

"Tyler," said Harvey. "I can't leave him." He felt her grip loosen as he stepped back towards the fire. He turned and was about to launch himself through the flaming doorway when, from inside, he heard the snapping of wood and breaking of glass.

A figure appeared, lit briefly by the angry flickering of flames and framed in the centre of the burning doorway. A heavy foot smashed the burning doors from their hinges, and they fell to the ground beside the group of men who had attacked Harvey and now writhed on the cold, hard ground.

From the flames, with the body of a woman lying limp in his strong arms, stepped Tyler. He emerged from the fire like the devil himself, his face a picture of hate, love and loss. It was a face Harvey had worn for many years.

CHAPTER FORTY-FIVE

"Lay her down here," said the woman in the back, taking control. She moved aside and let Tyler lay his mother on the carpeted floor of the Volkswagen van.

"We need to go," said the man at the wheel. Beside him sat another woman. She had a laptop on her legs and the screen showed a live satellite view of the area with icons closing in on one place.

The Golden Ring.

"In the van," said Harvey, and shoved him inside. "Go, go, go, Reg." Harvey stepped in and slid the door closed. He knelt beside Tyler's mum, refusing to meet Tyler's stare.

The van roared into life. It slid sideways out of the pub car park onto the wet tarmac, and Reg fought to hold on. Tyler found a hand-hold but couldn't tear his eyes from his mum's dead body as it rolled from side to side with the movement of the van.

"Get us somewhere safe, Reg," said Harvey, as the woman tried to find a pulse on Tyler's mum. She looked up at Harvey, and offered him a faint shake of her head as if shielding the news from Tyler.

"It's okay," said Tyler. "I know. She's been dead for a while."

"I'm sorry," she said, as she pulled a blanket from the small couch beside her. "You did a brave thing to get her out of there."

"No," said Tyler. "Don't cover her. Please. I want to see her. For a while, at least."

"How did you even find me, Melody?" asked Harvey. "I left my phone at the restaurant so you couldn't find me."

The woman in the front passenger seat turned to face the rear and found Harvey staring back at her.

"Easy," she said. "We just followed the trail of death and destruction. The police found a body in an old disused power station in South London. I found the satellite feed and video footage and saw you leaving with two men. I took the license plate of the car you got into and tracked its inbuilt GPS to the Golden Ring."

Harvey stared back at her in disbelief.

"You know you two really are made for each other?" he said. "Jess, how about you use those skills and get us somewhere far, far away."

They sped from Plaistow and slowed when they reached the relative safety of Silvertown's backstreets. The engine quietened and the sirens faded away, leaving only Tyler's occasional heavy exhales as he sought to make sense of the situation.

Suddenly, the car behind flicked on its full beam headlights, filling the interior of the small van with harsh light.

"Who's that?" asked Reg, squinting as the car grew closer and nudged into the back of the van. Reg barely maintained control and took the side mirrors off a row of parked cars in a spray of orange sparks.

"Open the rear door," said Harvey, searching for a weapon of some kind as the car once more smashed into the back of the van.

But as much as Tyler tried, the door wouldn't budge. The hits from the car had wedged it closed.

"Left turn coming up," said Reg. "Hold on."

A squeal of tyres, piercing and shrill, filled the van as it lurched to one side at the limits of its stability. Harvey wrenched open the side door as the car came in for one last hit, a hit that would topple the van. But Harvey launched himself onto the front of the car, as the van careened around the corner, taking out two more parked cars and barely making the turn.

The van rolled to a stop as everyone inside looked back in horror. The speeding car had made no attempt to turn or stop. It smashed through the two parked cars, tore down an iron safety barrier onto wasteland and launched off a pile of rubble. Its engine roared and the wheels span uselessly before the front of the car plunged into the inky-black water of the River Thames.

Only the idling rumble of the van's engine could be heard as everyone took in the sight and feared the worst.

Tyler was up and out of the van before anybody spoke. Inside him, as he ran, a warm, familiar feeling clawed its way from the very pit of his stomach, through his chest and found solace in Tyler's mind.

The car was gone, completely submerged. Only the headlights shone with fading enthusiasm, which then disappeared as the car sank to the river's depths.

Tyler pulled off his top mid-run. He threw it to the side and began to kick off his trainers when Melody tackled him to the ground.

"No," she said. "Don't be stupid."

But he rolled her away and sprang to his feet, just before Reg and Jess took him down in a joint effort. He struggled, but Melody joined them, and together, they pinned him down.

Inside, the beast roared. It kicked out at Reg, sending him flying backwards. Melody dove on top of Tyler's free leg as the beast threw Jess away like a rag doll. But as he reached for Melody, she twisted his leg. A pulse of anger flashed through his eyes and he kicked out violently.

Melody was ready for it. She moved to one side, collected both legs and bound them together with her belt. Tyler lay face down, his legs forced up and back by Melody's surprising strength. His face was forced into the mud and gravel.

"Let him go," she said, her face beside his. His arms tensed with the raging beast inside him, seeking a way out. But it was futile. "Let him go."

A coolness washed over his face, leaving only burning tears behind his eyes as the beast sank back to the depths. His muscles relaxed and grief overcame him. With the anger gone, Melody released her belt and dropped down beside him. He rolled to one side to look at her. Reg and the other girl stood on the river bank calling out Harvey's name. But Melody seemed content to sit with her legs tucked up to her chest with her arms wrapped around them.

"Let him go," she whispered once more, as if the words she had spoken had been shared for them both.

CHAPTER FORTY-SIX

A dark sky loomed ahead and in front, lit only by the ambience of a hundred million lights scattered across the City of London and beyond. At the peripherals of his vision, the world passed like looped scenery and faded away before any focus of vision determined its nature, purpose or identity.

Travelling at the whim and mercy of the moonlit tides, with only the breath in his body to keep him afloat, he lay calm and still and contemplated life itself in waves of guilt, loss and shame. Each memory held the touch of an angel. Each was a step closer to heaven and the closing of heavy, dark doors.

A searing pain jabbed at his leg, but there was no need to reach down. He'd felt the sharp shard of bone split his skin the moment the car had hit the water. The current was strong and, for a brief moment, he considered using his arms to take him to the shore. But a warm feeling of closure accompanied the idea of floating out to sea. To be swallowed whole by nature's most fearsome weapon. To die silently beneath a sky of stars.

The river widened as it neared the estuary and its shallow waves rushed up onto the nearby mud flats then broke with a rhythmic percussion. Two strong hands hauled him from the water and onto the deep muddy banks where they dropped him beside a rotted, wooden post that maybe, one day, in a time long forgotten, formed part of a jetty. Now it sat alone, exposed by the moon and its tides, waiting for the river to return to full height.

He closed his eyes, and as the cold wind rushed across the River Thames, sending his body into uncontrollable spasms of shivers, he was lulled to somewhere warm. It was a memory of fire and death, where distant screams hung like haunted voices, and chaos ensued at the centre of a rioting mass of charred and burnt human forms.

But it was warm.

He woke to the kiss of lapping water by his side while behind him, two heavy boots slipped and stomped in the thick, dark mud. Any inquisitive thoughts as to who, why or how succumbed to his desire to let the river wash him away along with the guilt, loss and shame that still stained his thoughts. The devil's hand still warmed his shoulder while the rest of him succumbed to shivers.

"You don't need to do this," he said, as a leather belt was passed around his neck and fastened with two sharp jerks to bring it tight. "You should have left me in the river. I'm ready for it."

The shivers set in as fits of body-shaking convulsions forced his body to stay alive, while his mind was far out to sea.

"I considered it," came the reply.

"So why didn't you?"

There was a silence as an answer was sought.

"I considered taking the journey with you."

"So why didn't you?" he replied. "What better way to go than on your own terms with darkness above and darkness below, and nothing but the whispering wind to hear your confessions?"

The boots slopped in the mud and stopped beside him. A dark shape loomed above, blacker than the night's polluted sky.

"I wanted to see you die," came the reply.

He laughed, a single laugh that sounded more like a breath.

"I can't remember the last time I laughed," he said, and rested his head on the rotted, wooden post behind him. "It's funny. It's only when the end is near that you realise these things."

There was no reply, just the shape above him and beside him, unmoving.

"How about you?" he said. "Who gets to watch you die? Surely there's someone who deserves to see that show?"

"I could fill a room with people who deserve to watch me die, John," said the man.

"So why don't you join me?" he said, and reached for a rock beside his leg at the limit of his constraint. It sucked at the mud as he dragged it close, and jarred when it found exposed bone. He breathed once, long and deep, then rolled it onto his lap. "Pull up a rock. The tide's coming in."

But the dark shape beside him had vanished, and the cool bite of the water washed over his legs, broke, and then ran back to the river. With each wash of the water across his body, a renewed energy shook him with vigour as still, his body fought to stay alive while his mind welcomed the rising tide.

He called out to the night but only the wind replied, seeking his confession with its whispering promise of death. With each whisper, the water rose higher, until it licked at the skin on his face, then receded to allow one more memory, one more confession and one more burst of lonely tears to leave him.

At last, there were no more memories, no more stories of horror to confess, and his last remaining tear was washed away with the tide that swallowed him.

CHAPTER FORTY-SEVEN

The avenue of trees shielded the small congregation of mourners who stood beside the open grave among the fortunate dead, whose lives were celebrated and marked with statues of angels. The mood was sombre but few tears fell. Each member of the congregation waited patiently to shake Tyler's hand or offer the estranged boy a hug before walking away and disappearing into the maze of graves. The minister was the last to leave. He placed his hand on Tyler's shoulder and spoke a few unheard words. Tyler gazed past him into the hole in the ground, searching for some kind of answer, or a clue to where his life should lead.

The fact was cold but true; he was free now to go wherever his heart would take him. He was no longer bound by the restraints of his dying mother. He was no longer the lifeline that brought her food and water, and worked to keep her warm and safe. He was no longer the lifter of spirits in those hideous dark days. The days when death had stepped closer and teased her until she tore at her skin with savage nails, frustrated, agonised, and tortured to the point of despair.

But that wasn't how she should be remembered.

She deserved more. She was more than a dying woman who had

demanded for her son to grow into a man, denying Tyler the final part of his childhood. She had been beautiful. The photos in their flat were proof that she was once full of vibrant life, strong and resilient. That was how she should be remembered.

The minister, with his hands folded respectfully, stepped away with silence and grace, leaving Tyler to share a few silent moments with his mum. Remembering the good times, the laughs and her beauty, he stepped forward and fell to his knees. He closed his eyes, searching for a connection. A sign. Anything.

He raised his face to the grey sky above, but no sunbeams broke through the clouds to warm his skin. Just the rustle of leaves and the distant hum of the city behind the walls of the cemetery.

He spoke his last goodbye then rose, turned and walked away. His lower lip was hidden beneath his front teeth and his eyes were narrow and dark. He was channelling the emotion, sending it to the pit of his stomach where the beast slept. One day, when the time was right and the beast opened its eyes, he would feed off that emotion. It would grow in size and strength, tamed, but deadly if not controlled.

Familiar with the maze of the surrounding graves, Tyler took a slow walk past Mary, the angels and Jesus, who regarded him, unafraid, like an old friend. An old Celtic cross dating back to the eighteenth century, with two hundred years of moss and mould embedded into its hard surface, marked the turn. Soon enough, Tyler stood in front of his father's bland grave marker. Only the other names of the shunned were witnesses to his grief.

Once more, Tyler dropped to a crouch, then fell forward to one knee. His hand reached out to stop his fall and found the soft dirt that he'd so often cleared of weeds. His head fell forward too as if the muscles had succumbed to its weight. Then the tears came. They rolled across his tired skin, finding the lines on his face formed by sleepless nights, and channelled into a single drip, which fell onto the factory-stamped letters that formed his father's name.

Julios Saville.

He sat for a long time in that position, hunched above a hidden memory of his father, and fighting for an image of them both together. He longed for a memory of his family, one of laughter and love. The image remained hidden if indeed it had ever existed. Only a reel of old photos played on repeat in his mind.

Never before had Harvey felt such a connection to someone. Never before had he wanted so much to reach out and help somebody grieve as he had grieved and to share the burden of loss.

A hand gripped his suit jacket. Another found the thin material of his new shirt and traced the outline of his chest with soft fingers. Her head fell against his back, letting him know she was there if he needed her.

Something stirred inside his chest. It wasn't the familiar, cold, sharp claws of the beast, but a warm, silky energy that found his veins and a single tear formed in the corner of his eye. His arm reached out, sliding around her waist and across the smooth material of her dress.

"It's time," said Melody with a gentle squeeze.

Harvey didn't reply.

The End

STONE ARMY - SAMPLE
STONE ARMY - BOOK ELEVEN- CHAPTER ONE.

Headlights shone like two dying suns at the far reach of Gabriella's vision, growing closer, burning brighter, and blinding her watering eyes. It was as if a searing needle had penetrated her visual organs and found the sensitive nerves cowering behind. Beneath her feet, the ground rumbled, silent but growing in intensity like the rising chaos of a stampede.

She turned to face the sound of breaking branches, barking dogs and men's voices, which had raised to a fever pitch. In the darkness of the forest, Gabriella saw torch beams cutting the night, leaving no escape except onwards across the railway tracks and into the unknown.

A distant scream pierced the blackness somewhere far away. The barking of the dogs changed from the howl of an excited hunting pack to snappy snarls as they cornered their prey and pinned it to the ground.

"Donna," whispered Gabriella.

A faint cloud formed when she spoke as the night air met her warm breath.

Another scream sounded, followed by frantic struggles as somewhere in the darkness, her friend fought off the dogs. A dark image formed in Gabriella's mind of the German Shepherds she had seen prowling the fenceline of the laboratory. She saw an image of the pack, excited by the hunt as they tore at Donna's clothes, their teeth clamping down on her hands and arms, pulling her to the ground, their ferocity far outweighing that of the men who followed her with torchlights.

In front of Gabriella, two sets of railway tracks ran left to right from the coast to the mainland. Beyond the tracks, the ground fell away to fields and a forest columned by the night; dark outlines against a dark sky. Somehow, after her ordeal, the black unknown beyond seemed calm and safe in comparison to what lay behind. But something made her stand still. To cross the train lines and escape into the darkness would mean failure. But returning to the hunting dogs and torchlight men would mean certain death.

Some voices called out to others that they'd found one. Gabriella still pondered, undecided. A single gunshot into the air, followed by the lighting of a flare, marked the spot. The searching torches turned and headed that way, bouncing through the dark forest. The flash of the muzzle and burning flare found its way to Gabriella's watering eyes, registering enough danger to trigger the carnal instincts to run and find help. But fear of failure glued her to the spot.

"We got one," called a voice. "Find the other one. She went that way. She can't be far."

That voice. The voice that taunted Gabriella's drug-fueled dreams and darkened her miserable days.

A torchlight span in a wide arc close by. It shone through the trees, tracing Gabriella's path through the long grass and up onto the embankment where she stood, frozen to the spot. The vibration beneath her feet was accompanied by the grumble of an approaching train.

The heavy pounding in Gabriella's chest amplified the sound of her breathing in her ears. She could feel the drug working. Whatever it was, it fuelled the familiar rush of blood to her head, the invincible surge of energy that coursed through her body, and the trembling of what felt like every muscle in her body, holding her body taut like a runner on the starting blocks.

A man broke through the trees. His beam of light cut the darkness like a long, straight snake. The dark form was unmistakable. Broad square shoulders. His head cocked to one side. The swagger of a man who feared nothing.

That man.

He was different to the others. He was cruel, with a voice that violated Gabriella and the girls, and with eyes that did more than undress her; they seemed to tear at her clothes just like the dogs tearing at Donna.

His torchlight found Gabriella. It blinded her and fixed her to the spot. There was no need for words; she could sense his leering grin behind the light.

In the distance, the dogs silenced, and a group of torchlights flashed in all directions as they began their hunt for Gabriella. The dark man in front of her glanced back as if he was considering calling out. But he changed his mind and returned his attention to his quarry.

His prize.

Gabriella took one step back. Her bare foot found the track, cold and hard, but buzzing with energy like the muscles in her body that tensed and relaxed with adrenaline.

Gabriella held his stare. The man responded with a look, daring her with silent taunts to run and inviting her to him with unheard charm. He gave a flick of his eyes to the distant oncoming train. She saw his delight in the sight of her last remaining seconds on earth, half-naked, scared and broken.

"It seems to me that you have three choices," he said.

An agonised scream came from the woods behind him. But it wasn't a scream as Gabriella understood the word. It was more of the final, anguished wail of a tortured, dying girl, and a submission to death.

"Three choices?" said Gabriella.

She shunned the sound of her friend's death from her mind, seeking solace in the growing rumble beneath her foot.

"First choice," said the man, "you can run. You can cross those tracks and run like you've got the devil on your heels and he's mad as hell at you. But you won't get far. I know those fields like I know the skin on my hand. I'll find you before you even break for breath."

The concentrated torchlights in the forest dispersed as each of the men spread out to find Gabriella. A slice of light lit the side of the man's face, revealing a knowing smile that he had her all to himself.

Dogs barked in the trees to her left, where Gabriella had stripped and run through the freezing stream. The men called out, whooping with delight and joking that the last girl was already naked. Removing her clothes was intended to buy Gabriella time and throw the dogs from her scent. But the screams of Donna had stalled her escape.

"Second choice," said the man, "you can come down off the embankment. I'll give you my coat and I'll take you back. No-one will hurt you. I can assure you."

"Just like nobody hurt Donna?" said Gabriella.

But the man responded with a shrug.

Rounding the long bend, the headlights of the oncoming train swept across the trees, then lit one side of Gabriella's body. The rumbling beneath her foot intensified, vibrating through her body, and the sound of the horn broke the night as if marking her two choices. Run or return.

"And what's option three?" she asked between horns, shouting above the noise of the approaching train.

The torchlight flicked off.

In the darkness, only shadows and dark shapes moved. The headlights of the train passed by the tree line, lighting only the grass, the tracks and Gabriella herself, growing wider as the train thundered closer.

Another horn as the driver urged her to move.

The ground shook with a pulse matching Gabriella's heartbeat.

But she stayed.

A backward step would commit to the run, triggering the man and the dogs into action. A forward step would admit defeat. He'd take her into his lying, devilish arms and use her for the evil he'd been dreaming of since that first day. Then he'd kill her.

But staying offered her only real chance of escape, to a place where even he could reach her.

But death would mean failure.

Another horn, louder and longer.

The squeal of brakes as two hundred tons of steel anchored, spraying great washes of sparks into the forest.

"Option three," he said, appearing beside her from nowhere.

He smiled the smile she'd seen a thousand times in her dreams, in her waking tortured days, and now, as death held her in its boney grip. The surprise caught her off guard. She stepped back, and stood between the tracks, where he seemed to dare not follow.

With half his face lit by the approaching train, he leaned across to her with an outstretched hand. "Don't be stupid, Gabriella. Come with me."

But Gabriella smiled and closed her eyes, letting peace find her, bringing with it the calm that allowed her to focus on cherished memories. She searched through her life in just a few seconds. An image of her father smiling in his garden, as he stopped turning the earth and leaned on his garden fork to admire her, fanning himself with his wide-brimmed hat. Her brother shooting her a wink as he led Gabriella from their home on one of their many adventures. She would sleep in the car. Francis would drive, then wake her up when they had reached the location. Each time it was a different location, carefully planned, and designed to enthrall young Gabriella. Sometimes it was the beach. Sometimes Francis would park at the top of a hill to look down at the rolling forests below. They would sit and drink coffee from a flask, perhaps eat a croissant.

On one occasion, Francis had taken her to Paris to see the

Christmas lights, but the memory was snatched away before she could relive the moment.

"Gabriella," called the man.

Her name came to her as he haunted her last treasured moments on earth. The Paris lights blinked off. The images of her loved ones faded away, but without regret.

The train horn sounded once more, loud and urgent.

The beat of the tracks moved the ground on which she stood.

And the drug that coursed through her body woke every living cell, firing energy into every single muscle.

"*Gabriella*," said the man, his hand clutching for her arm.

Another loud horn. The headlights, as bright as the sun, held the two of them in limbo. The ground, the trees, the whole world, was white.

His outstretched arm.

Those evil eyes. Men burst from the forest behind him and stopped as the train bore down on her like a raging beast. She had just one-second of living remaining. One-second to deny evil its glory. One-second to cherish life.

"I die for France," she said.

Then ran.

Also by J.D. Weston

Award-winning author and creator of Harvey Stone and Frankie Black, J.D.Weston was born in London, England, and after more than a decade in the Middle East, now enjoys a tranquil life in Lincolnshire with his wife.

The Harvey Stone series is the prequel series set ten years before The Stone Cold Thriller series.

With more than twenty novels to J.D. Weston's name, the Harvey Stone series is the result of many years of storytelling, and is his finest work to date. You can find more about J.D. Weston at www. jdweston.com.

Turn the page to see his other books.

THE HARVEY STONE SERIES

The Silent Man

To find the killer, he must lose his mind...

See www.jdweston.com for details.

The Spider's Web

To catch the killer, he must become the fly...

See www.jdweston.com for details.

The Mercy Kill

To light the way, he must burn his past...

See www.jdweston.com for details.

The Savage Few

Coming 2021

Join the J.D. Weston Reader Group to stay up to date on new releases, receive discounts, and get three free eBooks.

See www.jdweston.com for details.

THE STONE COLD THRILLER SERIES

The Stone Cold Thriller Series

Stone Cold

Stone Fury

Stone Fall

Stone Rage

Stone Free

Stone Rush

Stone Game

Stone Raid

Stone Deep

Stone Fist

Stone Army

Stone Face

The Stone Cold Box Sets

Boxset One

Boxset Two

Boxset Three

Boxset Four

Visit www.jdweston.com for details.

THE FRANKIE BLACK FILES

The Frankie Black Files

Torn in Two

Her Only Hope

Black Blood

The Frankie Black Files Boxset

Visit www.jdweston.com for details.

A NOTE FROM THE AUTHOR

Stone Fist takes us straight back into the wild, gangland world of London. While just a few of the locations were real, the Golden Ring was based on a pub that I drank in very often during my younger years.

Cable Street is featured prominently in the story and of course the Highway. I love this area. There are so many back streets, alleyways and shadows, Harvey loves shadows. It's no wonder the area was a haunt for the infamous Jack the Ripper.

So now Harvey is entering a new era. With Tyler under his wing and Melody by his side what can possibly go wrong?

I hope you stick around to find out, because it's sure to be a wild ride.

Thank you for reading.

J.D.Weston

To learn more about J.D.Weston
www.jdweston.com
john@jdweston.com

ACKNOWLEDGMENTS

Authors are often portrayed as having very lonely work lives. There breeds a stereotypical image of reclusive authors talking only to their cat or dog and their editor, and living off cereal and brandy.

I beg to differ.

There is absolutely no way on the planet that this book could have been created to the standard it is without the help and support of Erica Bawden, Paul Weston, Danny Maguire, and Heather Draper. All of whom offered vital feedback during various drafts and supported me while I locked myself away and spoke to my imaginary dog, ate cereal and drank brandy.

The book was painstakingly edited by Ceri Savage, who continues to sit with me on Skype every week as we flesh out the series, and also throws in some amazing ideas.

To those named above, I am truly grateful.

J.D.Weston.

9 781914 270321